I0679062

B.D.PEDERSEN

CYCLERS

Edited by
Shannon Lynam
June Pedersen

© 2013 January Brian. D. Pedersen

All Rights Reserved

ISBN-13: 978 0692564622
ISBN-10: 0692564624

PROLOGUE

I find myself rather tired right now. The past few months have been a heavy burden on me and a lot of my friends have died during that time. My world has been significantly altered and it is now left to those of us who have survived whole to rebuild it.

Even now my mind tries to tell me I'm crazy. That what I witnessed actually did not happen, yet when I look out the window of my office, I can see the destruction right there in front of me.

Yet, this is not the end. No, we are starting over. The danger is what we have eradicated from our world is still out there, and may still be capable of trying to control us again. I sure hope not, because the next time they will be even more ruthless.

Hanna and I have a heavy load here at the Group facilities. The structures are all right, but the inner workings will need to be rebuilt. The Mid Atlantic Group was a career dream that would prove to be the start of my adventure and the war that was fought across the dimensions. Those who were under the Cyclers control have lost everything, those of us who were able to avoid their control, are now left to care for them.

You would never in a thousand years believe what I'm about to tell you, but believe me, if I had not lived it myself, I would not believe it either.

So please, sit back and listen carefully. How careful you are right now will determine whether you can avoid falling in to the same trap down the road twenty to thirty years from now. If our attack was successful, and did in fact destroy the Cyclers, then you have nothing to worry about, but if it did not, well that will be your war. For now, mine is over.

Heed this warning. Watch the mirrors, for it is by the mirrors that the dimension will come forth and take your minds and subject your lives to their will. Hear my story and then pass it on. Never let it drop by the way side, it will be as important then as it was now. Come let me tell you about it.

Just a few rules I want you to remember, they are important. Keep an open mind. Don't let your personal feelings get in the way. You must be willing to hear it all and then consider the evidence.

Once started, do not stop. You must read on to the bitter end. If you fail to do that, you will miss elements of this story that will be vital for your future.

Do not judge. Accept the fact those I refer to in this story were not themselves and certainly did not want to be dominated and controlled as they were.

Control your temper. When you lose control, you sacrifice your ability to think straight and clearly. Make every attempt to maintain your emotions; it will be vital to your future.

Now, commit yourself to reading this document and stay the course. Remember, you're simply reading it, I lived it.

Chapter One

CYCLERS

Cyclers, I had never heard of them before and I had no idea who coined that name. You probably have never heard of this before either. Once I was drawn fully into the issue of Cyclers, and their impact on my life, there was no way of backing out or leaving this thing behind.

Cyclers, they would change my life and it would never return to what it was before. My world was going to come apart at the seams and there was nothing I could do about it, so I engaged with them to fight to the death. As the new generation, you need to know of this war and what it really means to you and your future.

I guess I should go back to the beginning and tell you how I came to being a part of this battle for the survival of human kind. They, the Cyclers, were something that would drift into my life and slowly draw me into this seven-thousand-year-old battle. All right, let's get to the start of the story and see if I can clear up any doubts you may have.

When I was young, I heard about this thing called cycles. I was studying astronomy and concentrating on the Solar System. As I read and explored, I learned for the first time the Solar System actually had cycles. That is, it went through different phases over the course of a number of years. Once through those phases, they would start all over again.

Because of my age, most of my questions were probably a bit naive and too simplistic. But it started me out in a direction I was to learn would create an adventure few if any really experience.

Cycles, what did they mean? How did they work? As I looked around my home town, I thought I saw little if any effects from these things called cycles. And then I came to see one of the most obvious, that being the seasons. They cycled on a yearly basis. You know, winter, spring, summer, and fall.

But, why weren't the cycles always the same? I mean, at times the winter seemed to be longer and colder and wetter. Or, the summer would be hotter and longer. They were cycles, but not always the same. Why was that?

In time it became clear, but then it was troubling. What troubled me was the seasons cycling was dependent on the cycles of the earth and the solar system. The more I looked the more complex it became. Depending on which angle the earth's axis was in would impact the amount of light and heat from the sun and would in turn affect the seasons and the weather during those seasons.

Then I learned even the animals were affected by these cycles. When a bear hibernates, it is determined by the cycles of the seasons and the oncoming time for winter. Even having babies (cubs) were controlled by these cycles so most babies (cubs) were born while the mother was in hibernation.

Fish will migrate from the ocean to the streams they came from, and then start the birth cycle all over again. And, birds would fly south as winter approached and then return again in spring. Yet, some birds did not migrate, they stayed here. And, most animals do not hibernate. It was really confusing.

The moon, or Lunar Phase, would cycle

through the new moon, waxing crescent, first quarter, waxing gibbous, full moon, waning gibbous, third quarter, and waning crescent. Whatever they were for or meant, you could see them over the course of the year and they always were the same and in the same order. It runs through that cycle about every twenty-nine days, why? The weather isn't that way, but the moon is.

Then I learned the sun had cycles. Actually, it has an eleven-year cycle and it had to do with sun spots or sun storms. It was a cycle that seemed to be stable and always the same and it ran an eleven-year cycle. Why was that?

The solar system had cycles, sometimes called planet alignments. Some people planned their lives on how the planets aligned, and they even went as far as to which planets were aligned at which times and for whatever reasons. I didn't know or understand what that was, but I knew there was a cycle there.

Did you know the solar system will go around the center of the galaxy once every two hundred twenty-eight million years? That's a cycle too.

In addition, I learned the distance from the sun to the middle of the Milky Way was twenty-six thousand light years, and during the journey of our solar system around the middle of the Milky Way we are traveling at one hundred fifty-five miles per second. That's nine thousand three hundred miles an hour. In one day, that comes to two hundred twenty-three thousand two hundred miles.

The human race is loaded with cycles. As a child comes into this world it will pass through numerous cycles when growing up. That child learns to walk, talk, relate, and get an education.

Certain parts of its body change and mature as the years pass. When they reach a certain age, they start to have feelings toward the opposite sex. That is a whole new cycle, Procreation.

As the body changes and approaches adulthood, the drive to reproduce becomes more and more dominant in the male and female. For the most part they must, they have to reproduce and it's that driving cycle that keeps the human race, as well as other animals, increasing their numbers across the world.

The Circadian Rhythm, that is your twenty-four-hour daily actions or activities including your sleep time and active times, is a cycle so powerful there is no controlling it. It must be it has to be.

"Everything has or is a cycle; did you know or see that, everything, from the most obvious to the smallest, of any life form or activity. Even Global Warming and Cooling are cycles. I'm going to show you I'm not crazy. Cyclers run us and we are victims of their control. Cyclers are beings. Yes, they are. I saw them. They're real, believe me, they're real.

"I started learning about them when I was a kid. You know the weather, planets, moon, sun, solar system and everything I looked at was a cycle. Did I tell you Cyclers were a living thing, or beings? They are, believe me. I'm not lying, it's true, they live and they control us, you, me, and everyone.

"Have you ever heard of the Milankovitch Cycles? Really there are cycles by that name. Sometime around 1941 a Russian scientist wrote this paper on cycles of the solar system and sun. In his theory of cycles, he identified a number of sub-cycles each in their own way added to the complexity of our lives here on earth.

"He, Milankovitch, identified the Orbital Eccentricity, which is the deviation of an orbit from a perfect circle.

"Then there is the Axial Obliquity which is the angle between an object's rotational axis and a line perpendicular to its orbital plane.

"Also, he had determined the Precession of the Equinoxes which is to maintain coordination and explain the time from one vernal equinox to the next. An equinox is something that occurs twice a year, where the tilt of the earth's axis is inclined neither away from or toward the sun.

"As you see the positioning of the earth axis has a whole series of cycles the earth goes through while it orbits the sun. His mathematics was wonderful, but they contained errors, which was not uncommon in those days.

"The complexity of the math involved would turn a young man old today. Yet, he was driven in his quest to understand the effects of the earth's orbit, rotation and relationship with the sun and moon and other planets and how this impacted our environment.

"At first, they thought he was crazy, just as you do me. But now they have computers and can check his math, they find he was right in his description of these cycles. There were minor errors in his math and formulas, but once corrected, they determined he was right.

His cyclical description of the earth's weather and environment was right on the button, yet for years they berated that man and all along he was right.

"As for me, I'm just taking it a step further down the path to complete understanding. What we see and call cycles are actually the results of actions taken by the Cyclers as they control our lives. No, really! Don't jump to conclusions about me!

"I know what I'm talking about!

"Listen, you have to believe me!

"Cyclers are beings just like you and I. They have a way and means of keeping us from seeing them for what they really are, I know, I've seen them!

"Please, you people have got to believe me. I'm not telling a lie and I do know what I'm talking about.

"Please, how can I get you to believe me?

"What do you want me to do to prove to you I'm not nuts or something?

"Will you give me a chance to tell you

the whole story and not just make your decisions on a few issues that don't even relate to what has been happening?

"It won't take long and it will clear the air of a lot of confusion. We can then deal with it once I fill you in and you have heard and seen all my evidence. I know once you hear it all, you will agree with me. Is that all right with you? Just a few minutes, please.

"I know this is hard to believe or to accept, but I feel I am capable of bringing all the information you need to come to the same conclusions as I did.

"So, may I suggest we set this up like a classroom lecture? Let me present my case without interruption and then when I am through, if you have any questions, I will respond to them. Is that acceptable to you?

"It is! Good, then I can get started. Right now, I need all my files that are in my apartment. Once I have gathered everything together, I can get started. It is acceptable to me if you want someone to accompany me to my apartment so I can collect the files I will need.

"I can start my presentation in about two hours.

"If that is all right with you?

"Or if you prefer, I can start in the morning, whichever you want.

"You want it now; great, that it will be, and I will be ready. I just have to collect my files and prepare for the presentation.

"Thank you so much for giving me this opportunity Mr. Lattamere. It will be of great importance to you when you hear all I have to present.

"I need a car and someone to help me retrieve my papers?"

Phil looked up from his papers. "Larry, I'll go with you."

I looked over at Phil and then back to Mr. Lattamere. "That would work fine, shall we go?"

Phil stood up and walked over to the door and followed me out.

As we left the campus, I noticed a light gray car parked across the highway from the campus gate pointing in the direction of my home. It was not common for cars to park in that location, and because of my stress level. I thought nothing of it at the time, and I would regret it the rest of my life, as short as it appeared my life was going to be.

I had come to the Mid Atlantic Group, a think tank, about six months ago. That would have been March 1st, 2114.

I had hired on as an analyst in the area of scientific documentation and evidence. My name is Larry Manchester and I'm a trained physicist and had taught Applied Physics at my home town community college up till being hired to the think tank.

One of my first assignments dealt with the theory that had come from the Milankovitch Cycles documents from many years earlier, around 1941. That document would prove to be the one key element that brought me to the situation I find myself in today.

There was nothing special in this assignment. Basically, it was a reevaluation of the papers on cycles and the process of correcting a few minor math errors that had been incorporated in the original papers by Milankovitch. The writer had found and corrected a number of calculations and in doing that advanced a new view point on what Milankovitch was trying to present.

It was that new insight that got me. I had no reason other than the fact I had carried a considerable amount of interest in cycles when I was a young boy. I think the paper was just the thing that was needed to cause that interest to be re-born. A re-birth that I would wish had never happened.

Yet, I cannot sit here and tell you I was not excited about what I was reading and what it meant to me and my interest in cycles, cycles of every kind.

Who would have known what I would run across would be world changing and would almost destroy my life? It wasn't much, just a small calculation that resulted in a window into the processes behind cycles. Just a crack, a small simple opening, that I ventured into and discovered the deepest and darkest secrets of the human race.

We were not the freewheeling, free thinking beings we thought we were. No, the fact was our environment was controlling us in every aspect of our lives and that was done through cycles. These are the very essence of our existence and growth in this world of ours. Those ingrained processes that were created in us on that first day so far back in history.

At first, I simply thought this was a coincidence and nothing more. It would be just a chance thing that would prove to be an oddity and nothing more. Well, it wasn't. It wasn't just an oddity it was a factual observation that would lead me to the next step. So, I took it.

First of all, let's define what a cycle is. By definition a cycle is "An interval of time during which a sequence of a recurring succession of events or phenomena is completed."

As you look around you there are cycles involved in almost everything. The moon rises and passes across the sky every twenty-four hours. As it does so, it passes through phases from full to new and this has been going on since before recorded time.

The cycles of the moon create cycles in physical reactions here on earth, namely the tides of the oceans and even the physical and mental condition of people. Human cycles are most prevalent from our lifecycle to our reproduction cycle. It's all cyclical. Everything works in cycles. They had to see that, they had to understand.

We got into Phil's car and drove out to the main gate where the gray car was sitting and then turned toward downtown and my apartment building. The light gray car fell in behind us. At first, I thought it was an escort from the think tank there to make sure I returned.

I could not see into the car because of the tinting on the windows and it made no signs of being a danger. You usually related danger to a long black limousine. You know like the ones you see in the movies, by their size and color you know they mean trouble.

Just then Phil asked, "Larry, are you really, all right? I mean, they are convinced you're crazy and as a result you have jeopardized the reputation of the tank. I know they're coming at you hard, but there is a lot at stake here and they mean to be sure the tank is protected.

"You know any think tank exists and prospers as long as their reputation as a non-partisan organization stays intact. Right now, you're a real threat to them and that means they are going to come at you with everything they have until they're satisfied the organization is still on firm ground and will remain so."

At first, I was not really listening to Phil. I knew he was talking and I heard what he was saying, but my mind was running all over the place trying to prepare for a presentation I knew would mean my future with the group. "Phil, I'm as rational as you or anyone else in that place. What I have discovered is beyond me. I had no idea and still find it hard to believe what I have found is real, let alone exists.

"That's why I brought it to the department heads. I wanted some guidance in what I had found and they overreacted. The response was totally off center. I was more shocked by that than I was by what I had found or discovered. You were there; you saw their reactions, if anything it was crazy.

"Crap, they wouldn't even give me a chance to explain before they started calling me all kinds of names and accusing me of being crazy. If I had known that was going to be their reaction, I would have simply not brought it to them and would have pursued it on my own.

"The fact is I had been working on it on my own time and outside of the tank on and off for a number of years. It's at a critical point and I need some advice."

Phil continued to press the point while driving me to my place. "That was a foolish thing to do Larry."

"Just what the hell was I supposed to do?" I asked. "I was following the guidelines of the job trying to obtain a little guidance, that's all. Phil, what does it look like now? It may have been foolish not to bring it to the board, but it has turned out to be even more a foolish move to have brought it to them. If I didn't know better, I would think what I was working on was a direct threat to their existence and prestige."

Phil was quiet for a while as he continued toward my apartment building. "Yes, I see what you mean. Is there anything I can do to help you?"

I was not inclined to ask anyone in the place for help of any kind by this time. People were overreacting, almost as if I had found a great secret or something. "Just stand behind me. You don't have to commit to anything, just stand behind my right to express my thoughts and findings in a manner and by a means that will be informative to them and help in their understanding of what I have discovered. What no one understands is that I'm scared to death. This whole thing is beyond me."

By this time, I could tell Phil was really uncomfortable with what I was saying. "All right Larry, I can do that."

Phil drove the ten miles to my home and let me out at the front door. He advised he would pull down the block to the next parking space and remain there until I came back out. I left the car and went into the apartment building.

As I waited for the door to open, I glanced down the street and saw the gray car pulling over to the curb at the end of the street. As the door to my apartment building opened, I thought to myself there was something strange going on here. That car was definitely following us. I sensed they were not there for my welfare or for Phil's either.

As I walked into the building I looked back at Phil's car as he brought it to a stop at the other end of the block. The last I saw of Phil alive was his car pulling up to the parking space.

My apartment complex is a fairly nice place for a single man to live. It has a monitored electronic pass-through entrance to the main lobby. It's a good-sized lobby and during the day there is a newsstand and snack stand in operation.

In the evenings and nights, they are both closed. As you walk into the lobby you will see a number of areas with chairs and lounges arranged in circles, kind of like islands. A couple of the areas had televisions in them for gatherings to watch a sports event or something.

It was actually a well used area all the time. A person could go down to the lounge and find any number of tenants there enjoying a good conversation or watching something on one of the televisions. It was one of those places that lent its design and layout to any and all kinds of gatherings day and night year around. It made the place a friendly and easy place to live.

There are four elevators that service the building. The building is comprised of thirty-six stories and each elevator services a part of those floors. Mine is the second one, that services floors ten to nineteen. I live on the seventeenth floor.

As I crossed the lobby, I noticed a lone man sitting on a bench at the far end of the lobby. He was reading a book and didn't even look up as I approached the elevators. As I think about it now, I should have realized he was out of place. No one in that building I know of wears a full brim hat.

I entered my elevator and went up to the seventeenth floor. My apartment is toward the front of the building and overlooks the street below. At this time of day there is little activity on the street. I reached my apartment and entered.

Now, I'm a bachelor and you know we are not the best of home makers, but I am really an exceptional housekeeper. I hate seeing things out of their place or out of order. There is a place for everything and everything has a place. If not, then that is reason enough for whatever it is to go. I keep nothing that does not have a purpose or a place.

When I left my place this morning at six thirty-five it was neat as a pin. So, what happened between then and now? The place was a mess. Damn, they wrecked it to the bones. Nothing was left whole and everything was torn apart. Yes, they had gone through my apartment, but even more, they had taken great pleasure in destroying it. All I could do was stand there. I didn't even think about anyone still being there.

I knew right then and there my day had gone from terrible to catastrophic without me having done anything at all. I should never have left the institute and come here. I could have done the presentation from memory, but I wanted the documentation to back up what I was going to say. All the work I had poured into that research, everything that demonstrated my hypothesis was right and factual.

Yes, you're right; it's all gone all my files and all my support documents. Even the computer had been cut open like someone had taken a can opener to it. Anything and everything that had to do with my research was gone, cameras, notebooks, files, and even my Thesis on Universal Cycles. They had cleaned me out. But who were they?

Who the hell knew I had all that work here, the tank? I think they could logically surmise I had a number of documents related to my studies. Was there anyone else? No one, it had to be the tank, but why?

I knew I had to get out of there and as I went back to the elevator, I remembered the man in the lobby and the light gray car that had been following us. I decided to take the stairs down to the ninth floor and then take elevator one. That way if anyone was in number two, I would not be walking into trouble.

My next concern was getting out of the building past the light gray car. I was sure the lone man in the lobby was already on the number two elevator waiting for me.

Wait just a minute. Who am I running

from or am I running into their arms? If it's the group, then I sure as hell don't want to run back to Phil's car and get in and be taken back there.

If it was someone else, well I had no idea what to do in regards to that. Who the hell would want to harm me? Crap, it was just a study and a discovery that frankly meant nothing to ninety-nine percent of the world.

As I entered the lobby, I noted it was empty and instead of going out the front door I headed for the back-alley door. Where else was I to go. Out the front door was the gray car and Phil and who knows who else may be there. No, it was the back door.

Dumb move, I walked right into them. All I can remember as I was falling was seeing the front end of the light gray car parked about ten feet away facing me. With that everything went to black, I didn't even see the one who hit me. Come to think about it, I didn't even feel them hit me.

As I came to, we were moving down the alley. At the end of the alley, we turned left and then turned left again, going down the street in front of my apartment. I was laying there in the corner of the back seat with my head turned to the window. As we drove by, I could see Phil in his car with his face plastered against the window. It looked odd the way he was positioned his sightless eyes looking out at me and a brilliant stream of blood running down the side of his face.

Why would they do that to Phil? As far as I knew he had never hurt anyone in his life. I had not known him long, but what I did know about him was that he was an easy-going guy who wanted to do his job and not make waves. There was no reason to do that to him. Damn them anyway.

By this time the back of my head felt like someone had hit me with a baseball bat. My head was spinning and I was finding it hard to concentrate. I tried to tell my arms to move then my legs and then my body, but none were having anything to do with me and my wants. I couldn't move, I couldn't think and when I tried everything went black.

As my mind swirled off into the unknown, I kept reaching out trying to determine who would do this to me and poor Phil. I was falling into that deep black hole and there was nothing I could do about it. So, I decided to let it come. I didn't want to be there anyway.

Chapter Two

THE ENDING

After seeing Phil, I must have passed out again. I have no idea how long we had been driving nor did I have any idea as to what direction we had been going. The inside of the car was dead silent. There were two men in the front seat, neither one saying anything. Next to me was another man and by his size I figured I had little or no chance of dealing with him in any other way but to cooperate.

I was able to tell we were no longer in the city, but driving along the freeway well outside of the city. It was a clear evening and we must have been driving for some time.

When they took me, it was around

seven o'clock and now it was dark and the sky was full of stars. How long have we been traveling? My mind couldn't grasp the issue of time right then, it was too muddled to carry out anything as complex as determining what time it was.

Just about that time the Big Guy leaned forward and looked at my face. "Hey, he's come around. How are you doing Mister Manchester?"

What the hell, he knew my name. I was trying to bring myself to a point where I could determine what was going on or at least get myself to a point where I could ask a question or two. All I could think to ask was, "Who are you people?"

The Big Guy was settling back in his seat again. "Not to worry Mister Manchester, we're just taking you to a safe place. It shouldn't be too long now."

As the fog continued to clear away from my head, I started taking a closer look at the inside of the car and the road outside. After everything that had happened in the last few minutes or since we left the Tank that was one hell of a stupid question. "What do you mean a safe place?"

The Big Guy just seemed to be of the

opinion this was just a simple day and nothing of any issue was involved. "You're going to a place where no one can harm you or be a threat to you."

Now I was getting mad. No, I was mad as hell and wanted some answers and I wanted them now. "What the hell do you mean? Harm me or be a threat to me, what the hell are you talking about? You already busted my head. You tossed me into this car and you killed my friend. On top of all that, what if I don't want to go? What if I tell you you're full of crap and you had better let me out of this car now?"

The Big Guy sat there looking out the front window, resting his huge hands on his knees. "I guess no one asked you if you wanted to or not, now did they? Just sit back and relax and we will tell you when we're there. Oh, are you hungry?"

I wanted to slap the crap out of him right then. "What, this is crazy you have got to be out of your ever-loving mind. No, I'm not hungry. I want to know what is going on and where you are taking me."

Big Guy just sat there. Nothing seemed to bother him. If I didn't know any better, I'd say he was retarded. "Mister Manchester,

Larry, this whole situation will be explained to you in due time, but for right now it's best you just sit there quietly and enjoy the ride."

By this time, I was out of my head mad. What was going on, I knew I was in trouble, but by whom? Then it hit me, "Are you Cyclers? Are you from the Cyclers?"

Big Guy looked over at me and shrugged his shoulders. "Don't know what you're talking about Larry. We're just taking you to a safe place and making sure nothing happens to you."

There was no use in my throwing myself at him like I had been. This guy wasn't going to tell me anything, so I came at him from a different direction. Maybe, just maybe he had feelings or something like that. Finally, I asked, "Why did you kill Phil?"

Big Guy looked at me and then back out the side window. "Who's Phil?"

I was exasperated by this time. It was like talking to a board; he just sat there and played the dumb card. "He's the man you left back in the car, dead."

Big Guy didn't look at me or acknowledge I was even there. "Oh, Phil, we don't know what you're talking about Larry. We saw no Phil, nor did we kill anyone. You must have imagined it."

This was clearly a waste of time trying to communicate with this thick-headed idiot. This guy just can't be real, what the hell anyway. "Are you human?"

Big Guy just stayed the road and played the part of the dumb guy. "Larry, we're as human as you are. We don't know what you're talking about and frankly could care less. So, sit back and relax. You'll learn everything you need to know in time. It's just a matter of time."

I was sure I was not going to get anything out of this guy no matter how many times I asked. He was playing the dumb card, but I could tell he was more complex than he was letting me see. He was well trained and knew full well what I was talking about and still he held his course and let me stew in my own anger.

The car continued on through the country side seeming to never come upon any other traffic or centers of population. I don't have any idea as to how long we traveled, it just seemed like forever.

There was the dead, unending hum, of the tires on the roadway. This was crazy. What the hell had I got myself into anyway? I figured I was not in danger of being killed. After what they did to Phil, I figured they would have had no qualms doing that to me right then and there if they were not under order to take me some place.

Finally, I felt the car start to slow down. I sat up and looked out the window and watched as we turned off the highway onto a secondary road. I saw no road signs so I had no idea where we were. You would think there would be road signs somewhere, but there were none.

We traveled maybe another three miles and came to a gravel road that turned off to my left. It looked like a logging road, but the gravel surface was too flat and level to be any logging road I had ever seen. The road entered a forested area and continued on for another one and a half to two miles.

As we went around a curve, I saw a gate in front of us. It was a large gate made of heavy steel girders. I mean, this gate not only said no trespassers, it gave the impression if you did trespass it was capable of handling you without any difficulty. There was power behind that gate. As I watched it open, I could tell it was remotely opened and controlled by someone someplace else.

We passed through the gate and as we cleared it, it closed behind us. It crossed my mind if this place was so secret, why a gate that simply advertised something big was behind it. I hadn't seen anything yet, but I knew it was something big when I first saw the gate.

I had noted the forest had grown out over the gravel road about half way to the gate making a tunnel of live trees. It was the perfect camouflage. From all appearances the road was a logging road that came off the secondary country road and disappeared into the forest.

The road continued on into a valley and as we came to the end of the valley, about a mile, we came to the end of the road. It stopped right up against the mountain. As we came to a stop, I saw the trees and brush start to move and then swing open and a large inner door opened inward.

The car started again and passed through the door and continued down this seemingly endless tunnel. The tunnel could easily handle two-way traffic. I would say it was thirty feet wide and maybe twenty-five feet high. There were lights about every hundred feet. They were staggered so every other light was on the right side of the tunnel.

As I lay back in the seat and looked out the window, I noted the walls and ceiling of the tunnel were smooth as glass. They were not made of concrete. Well, it didn't look like concrete. Whoever did it or how they did it, I could not guess?

All I know is it was smooth and that started me worrying. Not that I had not been worrying up to this point. But, now a whole new list of possibilities was coming to my mind. My imagination started to run at full speed and it was not telling me anything I wanted to hear. It simply could not be that bad, please tell me that is so.

I guess I stiffened up because the big guy next to me told me to relax. "Larry, relax, we're almost there."

Yeah, right, almost there. If things continued as they have so far, almost may be another ten miles. "There? Just where the hell was there? And maybe I didn't want to be there, you ever get that feeling?"

All I could do was to sit and wait. I tried to keep from thinking. 'There'? What the hell was 'There' anyway? It could be a place to torture me. It could be a place to kill me, or hide me, or jail me or what-the-hell anyway.

I was even surer now I was being held by the Cyclers. Yet, these guys didn't look like Cyclers, they looked human. Could Cyclers look human? Maybe they could, I'm sure I'm about to find out.

Again, we started to slow down and the tunnel made a gradual turn to the right and then entered the biggest interior dome I had ever seen. Well, I guess, it's the only interior dome I've seen. I've been to many domed stadiums and that's what it reminded me of, but it was inside a mountain and not the insides of a building.

It had to be three hundred feet across and easily a hundred feet high. There were cars and trucks parked along the walls and when I looked out the front window, I could see a complex of building that were against the wall and extended into the mountain. We were headed right for the central one.

As we came to a stop the big guy reached over and put his hand on my shoulder. His expression changed to that of a father. "Now Larry, you're going to be a nice guy when we leave the car. All you have to do is stand up and walk between myself and my partner in the front seat.

"Please don't try to run or do anything

else, just walk and keep pace with us. Let me put it to you this way, if you do not do as I just told you I will have no other option than to immobilize you and I can assure you, you do not want me to do that. Now, do we have an understanding?"

I looked at Big Guy and then focused on his eyes and I can tell you I was going to do just exactly what he told me to do and not try anything. That my friend is what is known as survival mode and I was moving full force into it. Look, they held all the cards. I wasn't even playing.

Anyway, what if I did try to run or escape. It was three hundred feet of wide-open space across the dome to the tunnel. Then, it was another five, seven or ten miles from there to the tunnel entrance. At least I was going to find out who these people were.

The picture of Phil kept coming to my mind. All I could see was this guy, who had done nothing wrong, who had lost his life over whatever this was all about. Why? Why did they have to kill him? It made no sense at all.

As I got out of the car, I noticed the air was fresh and cool. Not cold, but cool and comfortable. I could not feel any air circulating around me. You would think any system that could generate that level of environment would or could be heard, but there was no sound at all. Not even the sound of vehicles or any machinery. It was so quiet it was creepy.

When we got to the building the big guy opened the door for me and I walked through. We entered a lobby that had to have come right out of a 1950s movie. It was long and high and wide with the deepest carpet I had ever walked on. The same coolness was present as was the silence. There were chairs and lounges spread out over the entire area of the lobby.

There was only one person there and she was sitting behind a desk as we walked up to it. She was a stately woman with long black hair and a soft rounded face. Her eyes were watching and searching at the same time. She knew why we were there and seemed to have complete control over herself and the job she was there to do.

My escort, Big Guy, approached the desk and announced. "Mister Manchester is here Sue."

Sue looked at me like she was looking at a new kid coming into the classroom for the first time. I would say that in the five seconds she looked at me she could probably tell you the size of my clothes, including my shoes, and in addition my height and weight. She nodded at me. "Have a seat, Larry."

I looked in the direction of her head nod and walked over to the chair and sat down. At that point, if she had asked me to lie down on the floor I would have. I was no longer fearful, but was now more curious and becoming even more so as time passed.

Sue picked up the phone and made a call. Sue waited a few seconds and then it was obvious someone had answered the phone. "He's here."

With that, she hung up. She told me he, whoever he was, would be out to meet me in a few minutes. I sat there maybe five minutes when the large door behind Sue opened and a short meek looking man came into the lobby. Big Guy did a half bow, turned and walked off, not saying a word.

The small man stood there looking at me while Sue handed him a folder. It was obvious the folder was about me or something in relationship to me. He walked around the desk and over to where I was seated and offered his hand to shake. I did not feel anywhere near receptive to any advancement to be polite or welcoming from this person and decided not to shake his hand.

The man withdrew his hand and referred back to the folder. "Mister Manchester, I truly am happy to meet and see you for the first time. I hope my people were not too hard on you. Please, would you follow me?"

That was it for me and I thought I could handle this guy anyway. "Who are you?"

He stopped and looked surprised, "Oh, I'm so sorry, my name is Carl Longstone, and I am your greeter and guide. Please, come with me." He turned and started for the high doors he had come through.

I still felt I had some semblance of control in this situation and pressed my position. "Mister Longstone, what am I here for and what is going on? Why was Phil killed and who were those men?"

"Those gentlemen?" Carl looked at me. "Hold on Mister Manchester, I understand your concern and interest in what is happening, but this is not the time or place for them to be addressed. All of your questions will be answered in due time. For the time being I must ask you to refrain from any further inquiry until the proper time and place."

That set me off. What the hell anyway, I had been knocked out and dumped into a car and hauled God knows how many miles to this place and for what I had no idea. Damn it anyway, to top it off my co-worker Phil has been brutally murdered and he's telling me to calm down. That's a bunch of bull.

I was building up a head of steam by this time. I felt, if necessary, I could handle Mister Longstone without any difficulty. Yeah, I was going to do that, and then what?

Longstone turned and looked at me for a few seconds. "Please, Mister Manchester, please. This will get you nowhere and it can only extend the time before your questions are answered. So, please, calm down and follow me. Everything will be answered at the time they really need to be. Up to this point you have cooperated just fine. Now is not the time to become difficult. Now, come with me, please."

He then turned and walked back to the big door and stood there holding it open. I got up and walked through the door into a long hallway. Mister Longstone walked off ahead of me, just as if he had nothing to worry about. As it would turn out, he had nothing to worry about. I was not going to do anything stupid at this time.

The area we were in was not unlike the offices at the Think Tank. I would guess we walked down that hall maybe a hundred fifty feet when we came to a Tee. We turned left and walked another seventy-five feet to a set of double doors.

When he opened the doors, we entered a large room that was maybe seventy-five by fifty feet in size. At the far end was a table with a large number of items stacked on it. Yeah, they were my belongings from my apartment.

He pointed me to a lone chair sitting in the middle of the room and lit by an overhead light. As I sat down, I noted there were chairs set around the room at intervals of maybe fifteen to twenty feet, each one with its back to the wall and facing me.

What are you supposed to think while sitting in a place like this? On a table not forty-five feet from me were all my belonging set out in neat order, each piece of paper neatly stacked on top of the one below it. Everything arranged in what appeared to be perfect order. It was almost ghoulish looking at it.

Someone had taken a lot of time and put in a lot of effort to set this place up just for me, and for a particular reason. Still, I had no idea as to who these people were or what their purpose was. It was obvious they were well organized and well-funded, but what side they were on was still a mystery.

My mind was racing over the past few weeks trying to find and identify those times and places where I had made significant findings in my research of the Milankovitch papers. What had been the key that had brought me face to face with the Cyclers? Most importantly, which side am I about to come face to face with, the government or the Cyclers, or were they one in the same?

Calm down. You can't think and rationalize when you're all upset. Just slow down and let your heart regain a regular beat. Think positive, something good has to come out of this, I hope. Be clear and keep your scientific composure intact. Do not give them the pleasure of knowing you're about to lose it all.

My instinct was telling me to control myself. Everything was going to depend on the next few minutes and how I handled myself. This was not a game; it was far and away beyond anything I had ever experienced before.

Just then several doors started to open around the room. Through one came a woman about thirty-five years of age, she walked over to a chair and sat down, not looking at me or even recognizing the fact I was there.

Another woman came through another door and then two men and then several more men and women. Each one walked over to a specific chair and took their seat. None acknowledged my presence.

A short time later an older man came through the door at the far end of the room, he walked up to the table and started looking over my belongings. As his hands passed over the papers and items, he paused and picked up the hard drive from my computer. He looked it over and then set it back down. After several minutes of this he turned and started to walk toward me.

He was a big man and powerfully built as well. As he approached me, I got a good look at his hands and I can tell you they were the biggest pair of hands I had ever seen. If he hit you with those hands, you would know it whether they were opened or closed in a fist.

The fist would probably kill you.

I felt myself brace as he approached. It was obvious something was about to take place and I was the focal point of it. I found myself bracing, preparing for whatever it was this person had in mind.

He stopped in front of me and stood there looking at me. "Mister Manchester, I'm sorry we had to bring you here in the manner we did. But it was vital you came here and you help us out."

Help them out, gees they have been helping themselves from the moment I first saw them. I was unfortunate to be captured by them. "Just what is here, and who are you sir?"

He looked down at me. "Oh, please forgive me, I forgot. My name is Reginald Hammerstrong and I am the director of this facility. I can understand your concern and anger in being handled the way you were, but believe me it was all necessary and vital we brought you here with as little resistance as possible. Believe me when I tell you, you are with friends and we need you here.

"The others are my associates and you will get to know each of them in time. Right now, we wish to get to know you a little better than we have been able to discern in the past few weeks.

"We understand your desire to know what is going on, but right now time does not permit us to address that desire. Please, we ask you to be patient and you will be informed about everything in due time.

"Now, as we understand you have been employed at the Mid Atlantic Group since March of 2114, or about six months. Is that true?"

Damn this was getting ridiculous. It doesn't make any sense from my perspective, but I felt I had better answer the question and besides, it was not that important an issue. "Yes, sir it is."

He appeared to be satisfied with my answer and then continued. "How many projects have you worked on in that time period?"

Now we were getting into areas I thought were of a classified nature and involved my loyalty to the group and my ethical attitude toward my job. "I don't know if I can tell you that sir."

He shrugged and turned around and walked away from me about three steps and then turned back and looked at me. "Never mind, it's been just one, the Milankovitch papers."

Now I knew he knew a lot more about me and what I have been doing all my life than I cared to think. It was clear he was going somewhere with his line of questions, but just where I was not sure. "Larry, when did you first come across the Cyclers?"

That one stopped me short. I couldn't answer him; it just stuck in my throat. I looked at him obviously in a way that clearly let him know I was in trouble. I was either with friends or enemies and right know I had no idea which it was, and I was losing control and starting to hyperventilate.

He walked over to me and put his hand on my shoulder and leaned over. "Larry, relax. It's all right, we know about the Cyclers and we know what they're up to. But we need to know what you know as well. Do you understand?"

By now I was clearly fighting to keep my composure. He knew more than I thought and probably knew more about me than I cared to hear about. I felt myself flush and go light headed. I noted he waved his hand and just then two sets of arms took a hold of me and lifted me out of my chair and carried me out of the room. At that point I passed out.

I have no idea how long I was out. I woke up lying on a bed in what appeared to be an infirmary or a hospital room. I felt terrible. Everything had finally landed on me.

I was confused and scared witless and knew full well I was in more trouble than any one individual would ever want to be. Panic started to well up in me again and I had an almost animal need to get up and run. I didn't know where, just to run.

How was I going to get out of this? Was I going to get out of this? My life had been turned into a trash heap and I had nowhere to go and more trash was coming down on me. I wished to hell I had never heard of a cycle or the Cyclers. Damn it anyway.

Just then the door to my room opened and in walked Mister Hammerstrong. He came over to my bed and sat down in the chair beside the bed. He had a truly worried look on his face and was having a hard time finding the words he needed to set me at ease and explain to me what was going on. "How are you doing Larry?"

I shook my head and stayed silent for a few seconds. "Please, please tell me what is going on? I can't live like this. Someone, someplace, has to be able to tell me something, anything."

He stood up and walked to the foot of my bed and then back up to the head and placed his hand on my shoulder. Clearly, he was bothered about something and was finding it hard to get it out.

"Larry, I believe we made a bad mistake with you. It is vital we maintain security and secrecy as much as possible. With that no one, but no one knows everything about this place and what we are doing here. We applied that same operational policy to you and that was a mistake. Things have been happening so fast around here we are pressed to keep up with them.

"Then we discovered you and we knew in short order you would be dealt with by the Cyclers. It was our intent to avoid that and to get you here where we can use your knowledge and skill to our best advantage.

"Right now, we want you to relax and regain yourself and then we will sit down with you and lay it all out. Can you accept that?"

I started to shake my head no and then stopped. I looked at him and knew he was being straight with me and I nodded my head in approval.

He then sat back down. "All right, we'll talk tomorrow. Get some sleep. If there is anything, anything at all you need, want, or would like, just push that button there by your bed. Someone will be here immediately to assist you."

He stood up and pushed the chair back against the wall and started to turn. He stopped and looked back at me. "Larry, we're not the Cyclers." He walked over to the door and opened it, and looked back. "See you in the morning."

After he left, I laid there letting my mind wander. I knew I was in trouble, but from whom. Surely the Cyclers were after me, and he had said they were not the Cyclers.

Then there was the Mid Atlantic Group. Were they tied to anyone in the government, or for that matter to the Cyclers? They had been firm in their disbelief of my discoveries and were in the process of destroying my career at the time Phil died.

Now we have these people who are obviously well organized and have more money than any one group of people should have. They also oozed power. So much power, that I could feel it deep inside. Were they my enemy or my protector?

He said they were not my enemy. Right now, I had no idea. I knew for sure they were my abductors and they would be holding me against my will no matter what I thought or wanted.

I had to think this out and the only way to do that was to go back and retrace all of my actions from the day I hired on to the Think Tank to the present. I needed to determine who was for me and who was against me and right now they all looked against me, including the Cyclers.

It was time for a trained scientist to apply his skill and knowledge to the problem at hand. Wild and fearful thoughts were not helpful. It was time to review, weigh, and determine my alternatives. No more crying and accusing. Now it had to be straight logic and hard-core analysis.

With that I set my mind to working on all I knew at this point. If Mister Hammerstrong was being truthful to me I would learn everything I needed to know in regard to their relationship to me. I needed to develop some means of measuring the information they give me so I can determine its level of truthfulness.

I knew little or nothing about this group who had gained control over me, but I did know about the Tank and all that I had discovered during my time at the institute. That would be my measuring stick when hearing their side of the story in the morning.

Chapter Three

MIND SEARCH

As I said before, I had been an instructor at a small community college. Actually, it was a small college in the town of Rockford, Illinois. Rockford is located in the upper or northern part of the State of Illinois

Rockford is a city of a little over a hundred fifty thousand population. I had lived in Rockford the better part of my life and upon graduation from Illinois States University I returned to Rockford to teach at Rockford College, teaching in applied physics.

In the five years I had been teaching I had been involved in a number of state wide studies and research groups and had done well. So well, that in January of 2114 I was contacted by the Mid Atlantic Group to consider accepting an appointment to their organization.

Now, in my field that Think Tank was considered a star positions a physicist dreamed of attaining. As much as I loved teaching, the call to Mid Atlantic was a no brainer. I simply had to accept and go, which is exactly what I did.

This was a career builder. From there I could go anywhere in the nation or world and find work in the fields and areas of my greatest interest. No, this was it. This was the greatest single jump in my career and I went for it.

So, on March first of 2114 I had my first view of the campus as I pulled off of I-90. It was the country setting I entered into that so impressed me. I had heard the campus covers something like a hundred fifty acres of land and that it was something to see. It was located about half way between Rockford and Chicago.

The first thing I discovered was it is a gated facility. I parked at the reception building and then walked into the reception lounge of the Mid Atlantic facility and introduced myself to the receptionist. Know what? She had been expecting me. Yeah, that's right, they were expecting me. That was the pinnacle, the top of the mountain I had just climbed. What else was there? I was here and that was it.

The landscaping around the entrance and reception area was spectacular. Stately trees lined both sides of the road and the lawns were a rich green and perfectly manicured. If one were to judge the prestige of the Group by the landscaping, it would be the highest of grades.

How can I relate to you my feelings at the time? Surely, I was proud of my accomplishment in achieving the appointment. Second, I would be working with some of the sharpest minds in the fields of science anywhere around the whole of the world. No, this is where I wanted to be and I was eager to get started.

After having my identity checked and confirmed I was given a map of the facilities and passed through the identification and document certification process. I returned to my car and managed to find my way to the main administrative parking lot, pulled into the lot and found a visitor spot and parked.

All right now what? The map they gave me was informative, but I was yet to figure out where I was on the map. Great, one of the smartest minds in the world and I can't read a map.

Several minutes later a man in a golf cart approached me, stopped and got out and walked up to me. "Larry?"

I turned and nodded my head. "Yes, I'm Larry."

He reached out to shake my hand. "My name is Howard Mitchell. It is my pleasure to welcome you here to Mid Atlantic. If you don't mind, we will be spending the day together while we get you registered and find your office and get around to meeting everyone. If you have any questions or needs while we're doing this, please let me know and we can take a break."

Howard helped me put my belongings into the electric cart and we were off to who knows where. In short order I was completely lost. Even the map wouldn't help me find my way back to my car. For all intent and purposes, I was lost completely, a captive in my career place of choice.

Howard was a fire ball and kept on going. "First of all, let's go to your office.

There is a pile of papers on your desk you will need to sign before we move on and start getting you familiar with this place and what we are here for and all about."

With that he drove along making half a dozen turns and swings around trees and flag poles until he came to a low-lying building and pulled up in front and parked. Five minutes later we were walking into my office.

Talk about an office. I never had it so good at the college. The office was at least twenty by twenty and one whole wall was glass and one of the side walls was nothing but book shelves and drawers. The desk matched the woodwork. The wall opposite my desk had a large mirror dead center and below that was a lounge. The flooring was a rich carpet that felt like it was two inches thick.

Howard was right about the pile of papers. It asked for the usual personal information, my direct deposit number and social security number and so on. Once all the paper work was done, there was a second pile of security documents I had to sign about things like, not taking anything off campus and not associating with anyone involved in a number of listed activities. A copy of each document was left for me to review in detail later on.

With that we then left for an in-depth tour of the entire campus before reporting for an introductory meeting with the owner/boss and his staff.

The campus consisted of a half dozen buildings ranging from single story to four story structures. They all had matching architecture, which told me they were either all built at the same time or they were working off a master plan.

It was a mind-boggling facility which included more office buildings, buildings with labs in them, dining facilities and a gym for the personnel to use either on company time or on their own time. It was immediately apparent the atmosphere here was informal and most conducive to the mental applications of those working here. Nothing was left out. It was a scientist's dream coming true.

They were fully computerized and had the latest in telecommunications capabilities. Everyone received a company cell phone whether they had their own or not. Most used the company system in that it was free and unlimited.

The resources were most impressive and I could not think of one thing they lacked as far as research necessities are concerned. Last but not least, I noted the entire campus was electronically monitored, probably around the clock and on weekends as well.

It took nearly four hours to make the whole tour. We then broke for lunch and after lunch we were to meet with the boss and his staff. I was a little nervous about this meeting. Probably because I was in the big time now and these were people who were high level achievers and they would expect the same from me.

As we were eating, I asked Howard what it was like to work here at the Group. He sat there a few seconds. "Larry, it is probably the most challenging job and place I have ever been. The people here are dedicated and committed to their jobs. Some are a little weird and you'll understand that when you meet them, and get to know them. I guess the point is every kind of personality is in this place and you will be working with every one of them."

We talked about a number of other things and then finished up and headed out for the meeting with the boss and his staff. From the lunch room to the meeting room was maybe a block and a half and we were pressed for time.

When we walked through the door the first thing to hit me was that everyone was there and waiting. I asked Howard if we were late and he advised me we were on time. It was a habit for the boss and staff to be at all meetings before anyone arrived.

The next thing I noticed was everyone was dressed almost the same. I mean, except for minor differences in jewelry and accent pieces, they were all the same, all seven of them, including the boss. I felt a slight tick in the back of my mind. That seemed odd to me. In a place where everything was set up on an informal basis, these people were as formal as any group of people I have ever met. That tick, was it an alarm or just a warning.

We took our seats and waited. It seemed like forever before the boss spoke his first words. He had been sitting there head down and concentrating on a stack of documents in front of him. He looked up, "Mister Manchester, welcome to Mid Atlantic."

All right, what do I say? I was told the place was informal, but the boss and staff turned out to be really formal. So, should I respond formally or what, "Thank you sir."

He continued on. "As you may or may not know, I'm Stanley R. Lattamere III. We hope you will find this job a challenging and rewarding position."

He hesitated long enough for me to realize he expected a response from me. "I'm sure it will be sir." I responded.

He smiled and nodded his head as he continued. "We here at Mid Atlantic feel we are part of one of the most advanced and progressive facilities in the world. Please, if you have any concerns or needs let Howard know and he will take care of it."

Again, he hesitated and again I responded to his remark. "Yes sir."

At that point he got down to business and addressed the whole of those present. "All right, I have here a number of new studies that have been received and need to be assigned. As I pass them around you will find your names on the one addressed to you or your department. Please get started on these immediately. Remember we have just two weeks to go over these documents and have a review ready for publishing. Are there any questions?" There were no responses.

That's when the Milankovitch Cycle came back into my life. I scanned the briefing paper attached to the face of the document I had received and then made a notation on it of the date and time. The second tick hit me in the back of my mind. Milankovitch, it had been a long time ago when I last worked anything related to his work, this may be interesting.

My attention was then drawn back to Mister Lattamere. "Are there any questions?" The room was silent.

He shifted his attention directly at me. "Mister Manchester, do you have any questions concerning the document and the assignment?"

I sat there a few seconds looking the introduction page over and then looked up. "No sir, the briefing was concise and to the point. I don't think I'll have a problem with it."

He then started to get more involved and specific in his inquiry. "Is the name Milankovitch familiar to you?"

Boy was it. This paper appeared to fit right in with my past history of research on cycles and their impact on mankind. "Yes sir, I've had extensive opportunity to study the Milankovitch formulas and findings. They intrigue me. The topic is one I have been interested in for years and I look forward to digging into it and seeing what I can find."

He continued to address me specifically. "Does the time frame appear to be a problem?"

Having not read the entirety of the document, that was a loaded question, but I addressed it anyway. "At this point it does not appear to be a problem sir. I will know more once I get into the meat of the document and extent of research it will or could require."

He seemed to relax and sat back looking around the table at each individual. "Fine, please, if you have any problems or need any questions answered get in touch with me or one of these staff members. Do you understand?"

What was there to understand, it was obvious that if I had a problem, I would go to someone with a little more experience in the operations of the group. "Yes sir, I do."

For a get-to-know-you meeting it was short and direct, and I did not get to know any of them. When he announced the meeting over, the boss and his staff all got up in unison and left the room. I looked at Howard and he looked back and shrugged his shoulders.

It struck me odd the way they got up and walked out. In time I would come to understand why. We got up, left the room, and I returned to my office.

My first official act as a new researcher for the Mid Atlantic Think Tank was to read the Milankovitch paper and make a series of notes pertaining to his findings and conclusions. I then took the new research document that addressed the Milankovitch paper and started to read it. It consisted of fifty-eight pages and appeared to be a credible piece of work.

As I read the document, I became more and more engrossed in the writer's research and processes. At first it was just another maze of numbers and calculations, but as I searched through the mass of figures, I noted a trend and a progression in his rational and conclusions. It literally clawed its way into my mind and slowly took over my interest in its contents. The mathematics involved was extensive and well developed.

There was something there that rang a bell. I could not put my finger on it right then, but there was something I was familiar with and it was important. There was that nagging feeling he had not gone far enough in working up the Milankovitch formulas and in not doing that, he had missed the mark he was trying to achieve.

Why he did not see it and submitted this paper without those final conclusions I could not say. But something was wrong and I was going to find out what it was. I had to. It bugs me when someone does a half ass job and this was one of them.

There was no excuse for the shortcomings of this work. What had started as a strong and elegant piece of work had become a short sighted and sluggish mess.

I'm not, a leave-it-at-work type personality. When something grabs my interest, I pursue it night and day, on the job or off. It made no difference, once I started, I could not stop and this paper had pushed my button.

I knew right then it would drive me until I came up with the answer. I was sure the writer of this paper had only gone half way. Why, I have no idea, but, he had not even begun to pursue the real issue behind Milankovitch's paper and rational.

That evening at my apartment my mind kept thinking about the paper and the research document. I was well versed on the

Milankovitch Cycles due to my years as a youth looking for and at cycles across the world and space in general.

The writer had left too many holes in his or her, work, and how the hell did I miss that one. Yes, it's a she. No, that can't be right. Most work I've seen from women are detailed and well worked up. The profession places a higher level of accountability on women scientists than it does on men and this one was a problem. Her presentation had made too many unsupported conclusions.

I had never read this person's work before, but if this was a true example of the quality of work this person did, then there was a serious problem and the paper meant nothing.

For example: in my own study of cycles, I had come to the conclusion that all cycles were related to one another. Even those that seemed to have no schedule or predictable process were related.

Once you accepted the fact, then the issue of cycles and their impact on all life, whether here on Earth or elsewhere across space becomes clear and more understandable.

Naturally, one is obliged to develop and

present his or her evidence as to the factual basis for that statement 'all cycles are related'. I had worked for years doing just that and this paper fell far short of that level of research and presentation.

Yet, it tugged at my mind. Why is this particular paper grabbing hold of me like this and pulling me into it? There had to be a reason.

All in all, it was a poorly written paper and I would bring that back to the board at our next meeting. Yet, within it there was a clear indication of a rather well-developed insight in the world of cycles and their impact on life.

As I sat there and mulled over the paper, it came to me this paper had been deliberately written in that manner. The author wrote it with the purpose of leading one to dismiss the science behind it. It was almost as if he, no it is a she, was fearful of saying or demonstrating too much. That gut feeling was stronger than ever. I just could not put it down. I had to follow up on it.

All that evening that feeling haunted me. As I went to bed it was firmly imbedded in my mind. At two in the morning, I finally got up, I could not sleep with that paper running through my mind. I could not shake the feeling the simplistic character of the document was not an accident, but was deliberate.

I should have recognized the alarm bells when they started to ring, but I was too much into the paper to let them register in my mind. Now, I can hear and see them clearly.

By then I was being pulled into the battle and didn't even know it. My emotions were all over the place, because I knew the world of cycles and my interest demanded I pursue it.

Finally, at four in the morning I fell asleep in my chair. I must have slept well because when the alarm when off I was up and going full bore. When I got to the office that Tuesday morning, I still had the paper on my mind and I went straight to it.

There it was, sitting square in the middle of my desk. As I stood there looking down on it, I noticed the name of the author. It literally jumped off the page at me. Not that I knew her or had any knowledge of her background or professional credentials. No, it was something else. Something about that name was familiar to me and yet not really.

I was standing there running my hand over the title page of the paper when I felt a presence. I looked up and Mister Lattamere was standing there.

I have no idea as to how long he had been standing there. I felt a little sheepish being caught flat footed. "Good morning, Larry."

I quickly walked around the desk to a position almost in front of him. "Good morning, sir."

He looked over at my desk and then around the room. "Larry, I normally drop by the offices of all my associates when I first arrive every morning. That way I can keep in touch with what is going on within the company. "How are things going for you?"

That was impressive. You seldom find the higher ups interested in what is really going on within their organization. I guess having his name on the ownership line of the group made him more aware of the fact those who work for him would make or break him. "So far it has been just fine."

He continued to look around the office and then right at me. "Have you had a chance to read the paper I gave you yesterday?"

I turned and picked the paper up off my desk and turned back to him. "Yes sir, I have."

His inquiry continued as he reached over and took the paper from my hand. "And, what do you think of it?"

This was my chance to let him know he had made the right decision in hiring me to work for him. "Well sir, from my first reading I would say it is lacking. I went over it in my mind last night and I am convinced the author fell way short of her intended target. If I had a student present that paper to me as a project, I would have sent it back to him or her and told them to complete it."

He was thumbing through the paper and then looked at me. "Larry, have you ever done any research on cycles?"

Good question, now he wants to know something about my background and capabilities. "Yes, sir I have. In fact, I did a complete thesis on the Milankovitch Cycles paper and have pursued cycles the better part of my life."

He looked at me with a rather surprised expression on his face, "Really! You included that in your resume?"

I was a little surprised myself when he said that. "Yes, sir I did."

He looked back down at the paper. "My associates did not advise me of that."

This was my opportunity to clarify the situation a bit. "Well sir, it was a minor project and not my master's thesis. I would imagine they were more interested in what I got my degree for and not some other minor works I have done."

That seemed to hit the mark for him. "True. All right Larry, thank you for your time and keep digging."

That was most interesting and I noted his total interest in the topic of cycles. "Yes sir."

After Mister Lattamere left I looked down on the paper and noted the name of the author, a Miss. Beatrice Melenkowskie and she was working out of the University of Illinois of Chicago. I sat down and mulled the situation over.

This was not a school that accepted half done or poorly done work. It was a strong school and had high levels of standards for its underclassmen and graduate students.

No, there was something wrong here and I needed to find out just what the hell it was. I made up my mind right then and there to call Miss. Melenkowskie and find out what is going on. But first I needed to know more about Beatrice and her work.

With that I went to the catalogs and started researching her name and any other works she may have published. I hit pay dirt and pulled her last published work before her cycle's paper. As I read the paper it became obvious this was not the same author who had done the work I had been studying. Her style was the same, but her detail and in-depth descriptions were far superior to this current work. Now I was convinced there was something wrong.

By the time I had gotten the background research done it was approaching lunch time. I needed some advice so I decided to call Howard Mitchell and see if he was available for lunch and to get some advice from him. He was and we met at the cafeteria.

Howard looked at me and knew immediately something was bothering me. He sat there and waited as I started to eat my lunch and prepare what it was, I wanted to say and what questions I needed answers to. Finally, he leaned forward on the table. "Larry, you look like you have something to ask me."

That brought me out of my thought process. "Yeah, Howard I do. I was given that paper at the meeting Monday afternoon and after reading it and reading it I have come to the conclusion it is a piece of crap.

"It was one of the poorest written documents I have seen in a long time. The problem is I did some research on the author and she is a top flight scientist. Her past publishing was not only good it was great. That runs completely contrary to what I have on my desk."

Howard was nodding his head and listening intently. If I didn't know better, I would say he was listening a little too intense. "And, what does that bring us to?" he asked.

"Howard, I feel I need to call this lady and talk to her. There is something really wrong, and I feel I need to pursue it. Is that something frowned on here at Mid Atlantic?"

He looked at me and started rubbing the back of his neck with his right hand. He looked down at the table top and then paused and leaned forward, "Larry, if I were you, I would drop this right now. Write your report and recommendations and leave it at that. The company will follow up with a letter to the place of her employment in regards to the quality of her work and that will take care of it. Its best you not get involved any deeper in this paper than you are right now.

"Look, Larry, we get lots of poor-quality work coming through here. It comes with the job and when it does, we end any processing of that work and refer it back to the organization it came from. Once in a while we will get a freelancer paper and in that case any criticism is referred right back to the author who submitted it.

"In this case she works out of the University and because of that it becomes their responsibility and not ours. You're not a teacher anymore Larry, you are an analyzer of other peoples work and with that you don't have time to teach them or try to assist them in their work. That is their job and not ours or yours."

How complete an answer could one ask for? It was detailed and directly to the issue. "All right Howard, I understand and I will finish up my recommendations and get another assignment."

A smile came across Howard's face. "Good, that is what your job is about and you will find you don't have the time to get involved in every single document that comes floating across your desk."

After lunch I returned to my office and completed my recommendations and submitted the paper back to the desk for processing, on the way I made a copy of the paper for my own files. By the time I was finished it was almost quitting time, so I decided not to commit for another paper at that time. For my first paper I was somewhat disappointed. I had expected more for my first task and it fell far short of that expectation. It's kind of put a damper on my being here with this new job.

As I drove home that evening, I could not get Beatrice out of my mind. There was something terribly wrong in that situation and I knew I could not just leave it. This was more than just the analysis of a paper written by a scientist. This was a paper written by a human being that was nowhere near the quality of work she had demonstrated before.

No, I had to do something and do it now. When I got home, I had almost completed my plan of operation in regards to my follow up on the Cycles paper written by Beatrice. I knew I would have to separate my activity completely from the Group and ensure I used none of the Group's resources while doing this.

My first task was to write down everything I could remember about the paper and the research I did on Beatrice. That is when I started my file on the Cyclers. I didn't know they existed at the time, but this would be the beginning of the process of my discovery, Or, should I say Beatrice' discovery and my follow up.

It was two days before I was ready to try and contact Beatrice. I planned on taking my lunch off campus on that day and using my old cell phone to call the University.

So, on that day I left the campus and drove downtown and found a small diner and took a booth at the back of the place and started to make the call.

When I contacted the University switch board I asked for Beatrice Melenkowskie. There as a long pause by the operator and then she advised I would be forwarded to the Dean's Office.

I sat there waiting and was rationalizing what I was doing when the receptionist came on the line, "Dean Singer's Office."

That brought me back to what I was doing. "Yes, I am trying to locate one Beatrice Melenkowskie, is it possible for you to put me in touch with her"

Again, there was a long pause. There was something wrong I could feel it in the back of my mind. Two long pauses and hesitancy as each one came on the line, "And, who is this?"

Things are always formal when calling into a university and this lady was no different, "I'm Larry Manchester and I was an instructor at the Rockford College. I have read a paper published by her and wish to talk to her about her findings."

Again, a long pause and then, "Please hold Mister Manchester, I'll transfer you to Dean Singer."

"Thank you."

What was actually a minute or two seemed like an hour. The time drug by and then, "Hello, this is David Singer, can I help you?"

Finally, someone who may be able to answer some questions and give me some guidance, "Yes, Dean Singer, my name is Larry Manchester and I am trying to locate a Beatrice Melenkowskie about a paper she had published a short time ago. I have considerable interest in the topic of her paper and wish to talk to her about it. Can you help me?"

There it was again, a pause. "Mister Manchester, have you ever met Miss

Melenkowskie before?"

Odd question, but reasonable, "No sir, I have not. In fact, the paper I am referencing to is the first of her works I have seen. It's just that I have been doing a considerable amount of study on the subject of that paper and I was hoping to see her about it. Is there a problem?"

I could tell this gentleman was having a hard time for some reason, "Yes, Mister Manchester, there is. Miss. Melenkowskie disappeared two months ago. There has been no sign of her in all that time. Her home, everything she owns was left just as it was and she was gone.

"She left the University that Friday afternoon and never got home. Her car was found in a busy parking lot, but there was no sign of her. Even her purse was left behind."

I was stunned and for a second there speechless, "Was there any signs of foul play?"

He seemed to be more distant at this time and I knew I was touching on something that was deeply important to him. "No sir, there was not. It is currently a missing person case with the police, with no leads. You, Mister Manchester, are the first person to inquire about her in all this time."

That really fired up the warning signals. I don't know why, but I knew in some way that paper she had published was tied directly to her disappearance, how I don't know right now. "That, Dean Singer, is disturbing to say the least."

The fact she has turned up missing seemed to tie into the paper and its layout and authorship.

I then asked him, "Sir, would it be permissible to come to the University and review the projects Miss. Melenkowskie was working on?"

I knew immediately I had touched something real sensitive. "Mister Manchester, I would have to know much more about you before I could permit that."

This was starting to get complex and I didn't need that. But, the more I got into this thing the more I knew I had to pursue it to its logical end. "I understand sir, and I'm willing to provide you with anything you need to prove my identity and support my field of activity related to her paper."

I could hear him thinking and knew I was on the verge of getting to the next part of my research. "All right Mister Manchester, I will see you. How about next Wednesday, say around two in the afternoon?"

It made no difference to me when or what time, I was going to be there, "That would work just fine for me."

He seemed to calm down a bit. "Then, it's a meeting?"

Great, I had made it this far, "That it is. Thank you, I will see you at that time. What do you want me to bring along to confirm my identity and purpose?"

He was prepared and advised, "Just your normal identification and if possible, a letter from the dean of the College you worked at confirming who you are."

I was in and the request was reasonable and proper, "I will provide that sir. Thank you and I'll see you next Wednesday."

Now I had to get the day off, even if it meant calling in sick. I checked and determined I had worked long enough to earn a day off and so I scheduled it. There were no questions asked and I was set.

Next, I called my old dean at Rockford College and asked him to send a letter to Dean Singer at the University of Illinois, which he said he would do and that it would be there by Wednesday.

I spent the evenings at home preparing for my meeting with Dean Singer. I had my copy of Beatrice's paper and was going over it in detail. It was clearly a poor paper, but there was something about it that caught my eye.

As I looked closely at it, I decided to spread all the pages out on my dining room table and then it became clear. It was a bad paper, but a great puzzle and it clearly laid out what would prove to be the main reason for my finding and seeing the Cyclers.

As I looked at the papers laid out on the table, I came up with a word that appeared to be common in the document and when I marked each one and stood back the combined word over all the pages formed another word. When I looked at "cycles" and marked each one, the word that could be seen on the table top was CYCLERS.

Another word that appeared common was "develop" and when I marked it and stood back the word it spelled was WATCH. Now I had Watch and Cyclers.

The next word was "common" and it spelled the word OUT. The next was "review" and it spelled the word FOR, then "event" and it spelled THE.

I took all five words and laid them out

to try and form a sentence and it fell together. WATCH OUT FOR THE CYCLERS.

What the hell did that mean by Cyclers? What were they Bikers, Riders? No, it had to do with Milankovitch and his study on cycles. Were there anymore words she had left?

As I studied the papers laying there, I realized there were others, many others. I finally finished arranging all the words I could find and the whole sentence was chilling. "Watch Out for The Cyclers, They Control Us, They Will Kill Us."

Clearly Beatrice has found something and as a result she had come up missing. Before that happened, she did her paper and sent it off to the Group. No wonder it appeared as a poorly written document. It was never meant to be anything else, but a warning.

What that warning pertained to was still a mystery and it would not be long before I was fully involved and fighting for my life.

Cyclers, just what the hell were they? I knew this, she had discovered something and she did it while working on the Milankovitch Cycles paper. That would be my key to finding out what this lady had gotten herself involved in. She was now missing and for all I knew dead.

By the tone of the message, I was sure by now she was dead. She had given everything to try and get this message out. Now I had to try and determine just what it was she was truly talking about. Was she just a crack pot, or did she truly have an issue I felt was serious?

I finished going over her paper and having found no more words I switched my attention to the Milankovitch paper. This theory was published in 1941. Milankovitch was a Russian mathematician and he felt he could explain the changes in the earth's climate through the varied cycles the earth, the moon, the sun and the solar system went through over the years. He published the paper during the early years of World War II and as a result it was lost in the world's pursuit of its self-destruction.

As I reviewed this paper it started to dawn on me, these cycles were way beyond anything we could do here on earth. They were cosmologically beyond our control and we simply lived by them. So, what was so important about cycles that this woman would do what she did? It was a puzzle, and I was not making any headway.

I sat there and looked over at the table with her paper spread out on it and then it hit me. The Milankovitch Cycles Theory was a smoke screen. It did not apply to her paper or what she was trying to tell us. She was using it to try and avoid interruption by someone or something. The question was who were they or what was it she was trying to avoid?

Milankovitch was an important study and it took the issue of cycles to the extreme, but it did not apply to her situation. It was a means of directing me toward something else. Something, any rational human being would brand crazy, not to be trusted.

I returned to the table and stood there looking at the pages spread out over the table top. She had 58 pages and, in those pages, there had to be a key, a clue to what she was trying to tell us.

Nothing, not a single thing came to my mind. I was blank. I knew the answers or means of my understanding what she was doing were somewhere on those pages, but I could see nothing. I stood there looking, wanting for her to let me know where to look, and what to look for.

I turned and started to walk away when it hit me again. Cycles, it was not about cosmological or global cycles, yet it was about cycles. The Milankovitch papers had caused me to concentrate on the types of cycles his paper addressed. That was the problem; I was looking for the wrong thing. Throw it all out. The only cycles left are those that impact humanity, life itself. It was living cycles, not cosmological or global cycles.

That was it. She had seen or found something that deals with living cycles. Those cycles that affects every living creature on the face of this earth and especially humans. It was environmental or biological in nature. Cycles none of us could live without.

Beatrice Melenkowskie had found something that dealt with biological cycles. Cycles everyone has and lives by. Just think of it, sleeping, eating, breathing, loving, intercourse, child birth, the whole reproduction thing, everything was based on cycles and if they could be controlled the whole of humanity could be controlled.

It was nothing short of staggering. This changed everything, it had to. Just think about it, you and I and everyone else on this world depend on these natural cycles for our lives. From the moment we draw our first breath to the moment we exhale our last breath; our lives are a never-ending series of cycles.

What the hell had she gotten into? Now I'm being drawn into it, I knew it, but I couldn't avoid it. I had to know what was going on and I was determined to track Beatrice down and determine if she was alive or dead. As I said before, I felt she was probably already dead, but I had to try just in case. So, the battle started and it was one in which I would either survive or not.

I felt certain what I was looking for was not obvious, but was in fact hidden and hidden very well. If I considered the term Cyclers, it had to be a title or a descriptive name of some kind. If she had been assaulted and killed then those who had taken that radical action against her had to be a physical entity, someone who was well hidden from the everyday activities of this world.

So, there I was. I had found the paper Beatrice had submitted was not simply a study of the Milankovitch Papers that was a ruse. Somehow, she had determined Cyclers was a name that referenced a number of individuals or in all probability a group or large number of individuals who were active in some kind of issue that involved humanity and the natural cycles we moved through during our lifetimes.

I sat down and let that sink in and give me time to really assimilate what I had just considered. Something inside me did not want to believe something as outlandish as a group of beings controlling the human race through the natural cycles, we as a living entity depend on. How could that be, just how could anyone, or anything, have that ability let alone the power to do something like that?

The only thing that came to me was a conspiracy and I had a real problem with conspiracy hunters. Just about anything and everything of any significance that happens across this nation and world is seen as a governmental or alien conspiracy. That was not going to draw me into this thing. If that is what it turns out to be then I'll deal with it. No, at this point the term conspiracy was as unlikely as the sun rising in the west tomorrow morning.

Yet, the means of her addressing these clues and the fact she is now missing give strong credence to the possibility she in fact did stumble onto something that was of a conspiratorial nature. That would be my mission, find out if it is and what it is. As much as I questioned it, I had no other logical cause to pursue at this time.

Chapter Four

THEY'RE REAL

When I got to the office the next morning Mister Lattamere came by just as he had done every day since I started at the Group. He did his usual thing, looking around the office and checking what was on top of my desk, "How are things going this morning, Larry?"

I responded in the usual and expected way, "Fine sir."

That seemed to satisfy him. "Good, do you have any questions?"

That opened the door and so I walked in. "Yes sir, I do."

"And, what is that?"

So, I went into my situation with the

Milankovitch Paper. "Sir, I finished the cycle's paper review and I'm ready to start another. Do I go to any particular location to get an assignment or what?"

His eyebrows went up and he looked right at me, "Well Larry, all assignments are handed out by me. Once you finish an assignment you are free to pursue any projects of your own concern as you, please. I have found that we come up with some rather interesting results when people are released to pursue their own interests. So, you will receive a new assignment this coming Monday, but until then you are free to pursue any thing you desire."

Gees, carte blanche, I could pursue anything I wanted to. "Great, there are a couple of issues that have always been in the back of my mind I could dedicate some time to."

He appeared satisfied. "Fine, follow your instincts on this and see what you can come up with."

My mind was already out the door and heading for the Cycles paper. There was nothing else I wanted more, and he just gave me the go ahead. "Thank you, sir, I appreciate that."

He could tell I was hyped by what he had said and that put a smile across his face. He would later regret that little conversation, but it was company policy. "Have a good day, Larry."

I was almost falling over myself when he left, "You too sir."

That was it. That was my permission to go after this thing about cycles that was driving me. I felt now I could devote my time to finding Beatrice, hopefully alive and well. My mind was literally flying trying to set up targets and priorities so I could arrange my investigation in to the mystery of her disappearance. That is not to say I would find some answers as to what it was, she was working on or had found.

With two days of free time, I turned to my computer and started digging into cycles. My main target was the biological cycles of the human species. When I opened the door, the level of human cycles was staggering. There were cycles in every human trait there is.

Upon seeing that, I thought back to the puzzle sentence Beatrice had made and it hit me. If they are real, they have massive means of controlling and directing the human race.

The question was, are they real and why would they want to control us?

Where there is control there must be a benefit to those who control. So, my quest was to try and determine what that benefit would be for the Cyclers.

Maybe that was the wrong place to start. How is one expected to determine the reasons behind a being's action when they don't even know who these beings are or where these beings are located?

To be able to determine their intent, you must have knowledge of the being or individuals formulating that intent. Right now, that was impossible. I had to determine the fundamentals first and it was to identify who Beatrice was fearful of.

When you consider cycles in this world, almost anything and everything is involved in cycles and depends on cycles for their existence. It is remarkable just how involved cycles are in everything we see, do, and think. Cycles are the foundation of our lives.

Some of the most important are related directly to our physical well being. Circadian Rhythm is one example. This has to do with our twenty-four-hour daily cycle and it impacts biochemical, physiological and behavioral processes of the human life, as well as other animal's lives.

The Human Life Cycle is tied to the twenty-four-hour clock starting with the joining of a sperm with an egg and moving on to the birth of an infant, then its growth into adolescence, into adulthood, and eventually in to old age and finally death. Yes, death has a cycle as well.

Social and environmental cycles provide the ability to meet a series of needs in physiological, security, emotional, social and spiritual issues. We simply would not be able to survive without these cycles. They are the foundation of all we are. Any life vacant any of these cycles is a life that has no purpose and no direction.

There are learning cycles, social being cycles, bio-geochemical cycles as well as carbon cycles, nitrogen cycles, and water cycles. Everything, and I mean everything, is controlled by cycles. The list goes on and on. It's never ending. On top of that, many of these cycles depend on other cycles for their existence. It's a wild menagerie of existences one on top of another and each fighting for its place in this world.

So, what are the benefits to the Cyclers

in controlling other beings? Somewhere in all these cycles there is something they need or want and that is what we need to try and determine. Right now, I doubt if we ever will. The bottom line is they control and have for more than seven thousand years. What their initial reasoning was is lost in those seven thousand years.

Why did I say seven thousand years? I sat there a moment and thought about it and then realized for the most part that is the extent of the human race survival on this world. It is in the last seven thousand years mankind had finally made its greatest expansion to the modern age. Still, I thought my zeroing on seven thousand years was a bit odd. OK, I'll deal with that later.

As I started a deeper reach into the issue of cycles, I started to have strange feelings coming over me. Part of it was the magnitude of the number of cycles that were turning up.

As I continued, I found there were cycles involved in every human function. I was beginning to realize much of what we do is based on what nature has determined. Then it dawned on me this may be where they are tapping into our system and gaining the control, they have held all this time.

Stop and think about it. Everything we do, think, or say has a cycle involved. For the first time I was really scared. She was right. She had found something that is beyond this world.

The shock of my recognizing that determination was overwhelming me. I needed to think about this. It was simply too much to contend with. I needed to break it up into manageable pieces and then deal with each one in its own time and own way.

I left the office that evening in a total state of confusion. My mind was running wild and would not slow down. There was something here and I didn't like it one bit. I stopped at the grocery store on the way home and got a good steak and then went on home and prepared it. While sitting at the table eating, my mind started to wander.

I had just experienced one of the most basic of the human cycles, the need to eat. It was a process that takes place two and three times a day and as regular as a clock. My body needs the fuel the food gives me in order to function, to think and process what I think.

For me to wonder was a good thing. I have found over the years my best ideas come up when I go into a wondering mode. I was mulling over the idea of cycles and those being controlled and manipulated in some manner.

Who could do something like that? Damn, everything ends in a question and no answers yet. The questions just keep coming and they're stacking up faster than I can organize them.

Who could do something like that? I don't have an answer for that question. The big question is not just who they are, but where are they from or at? It's obvious we have no idea if they're here or not. Who has ever seen one? Where would a being have to be in order to control us? Close by? Not in this universe, so it had to be dimensional.

It would be easy if that being lived here on this world or for that matter in or around this galaxy, but when they live in another dimension, what the hell. You have to have something to go on. Something that is tangible and logical. So that gives me two issues I must address, the possibility our cyclers are of another dimension and just which cycle or combination of cycles are being used. It could be just about anything, any force or cycle we have running all over this universe of ours.

No, we need to have a more in-depth knowledge of these beings before we can speculate as to why they do this or that particular thing. However, I can make a wild guess and I think it's for power. The power to control, manipulate other societies, other worlds, and other dimensions. I think that is a good probability. Well, it's as good as any other thought I've had so far.

If they do it because they need something that would guarantee their survival, then I would understand their drive to control us. But what in this dimension could be imported into theirs that would give them an advantage over their environment. I can't think of anything right now.

Just then a thought came over me that really hit home. There are books and verbal stories of human beings seeing and meeting beings that were not of this world. There are stories of gargoyles, giants, wolf men, vampires, monsters and strangers. Our history is full of these recordings or stories.

What if they were true? What if these beings, these creatures actually came from another dimension with the only purpose of furthering the control of the Cyclers over mankind? That opened up a whole new line of thought.

Slowly I developed my hypothesis. That was, the human race was in fact being controlled, directed, overseen, and dominated by beings of another world or dimension.

My problem was proving it. Second, if my hypothesis is true, then what was keeping them from knowing what I am doing and taking action against me?

That was a chiller of a thought. If it were true, they do control us, then it should be true they are aware of everything and anything we do or are planning on doing. If that is all true then, as of right now, I am in serious danger. Look at what happened to Beatrice. She was missing and she came up missing shortly after publishing her paper, if they took her, then why not me.

Yet, maybe I'm not a problem for them. How was I going to prove it? Did it matter to them whether I or anyone else tried to uncover their presence and actions against us? If they did, then Beatrice was surely dead. If they did not, then Beatrice was involved in something else related to this study.

Man, does that open things up. Every time I turn around, I'm coming up with another possibility. If I keep this up it will drive me nuts.

All right, where am I? I am sure this is real and there is a process of control over the human species by beings who were referred to by Beatrice as being Cyclers. That the cycles they control are those related to the human species, which ones at this time are not known. That in past history they have been seen by people in personal contacts or events with them, most notably, with bad results most of the time.

I finally went to bed and fell fast asleep. I was bone tired and emotionally worn out. I needed the sleep badly. It was around four in the morning when I was awakened by something. I laid there in my bed listening. It was a quiet shuffling sound like someone walking across a carpet with a gown dragging along behind. At first it was there and then gone, like someone taking a step or two and then stopping and listening for anyone in or around them. Like someone stalking another.

I had an urge to call out, but I stifled it and remained dead silent. I was positive there was someone or something outside my bedroom door and I was going to wait it out. Just then the door started to open. My bed was in a position where the light from the hallway, where I left a night light on all the time, did not cross over the bed and me. I was totally in the dark where I was laying.

It only opened a few inches and then stopped. I could tell there was someone on the other side. Its shadow covered the light that should have been cast across the floor. It stood there for maybe a minute and then pulled back and closed the door. It moved on down the hallway to the next bedroom and I heard the door open as well.

What the hell was it looking for? Surely it was me, but it did not come into my room and if they are in fact controlling us, they should have known I was in that first bedroom.

That's it; they don't know everything in detail. They control the species, but do not control and monitor each individual. That would be my ace in the hole. That made total sense if they were monitoring each individual, then this being would have walked right into the room and up to my bed. So, they cannot monitor at the individual levels.

If that were true then how would they know I was involved in something that was related or important to them? They would have to, in some fashion, have some kind of tracking system where they could detect and determine when an individual was in fact doing something that could be or was a threat.

If they cannot monitor a person directly then they have to use those they actually do control, but that doesn't make any sense at all. If they can't monitor the individual then how can they direct an individual to gather information? No, it's something simpler, it's a group. That was it, they can control and direct a group of individuals and in that way track the individual.

Then it came back down the hallway and again stopped at my door. This time it opened the door and flung it all the way open. It still would not be able to see me, but I got a perfect view of it. At about four feet tall I figured I could handle it if need be.

I then noted it was a woman, or a woman like being. I did not get a clear look at her face, but what I did see was not that unpleasant. She stood there looking into the dark and then stepped into the room. I prepared to fight for my life in the event she or it found me.

She had gone into a semi crouch with her arms and hands outstretched like she was trying to feel for me. Something told me to stay perfectly still and not to make a single noise. My sixth sense told me this being was dangerous and I would not be able to handle her after all. This being was not there for my welfare. I broke into a cold sweat and held my breath. It was a situation that gave me no outs.

Finally, it withdrew from the room slowly closing the door behind it. I was not able to sleep the rest of the night and stayed right where I was and remained as quiet as I could until well into the morning. Finally, I had to get up and go out to the living room. When I got there no one was in the apartment. The front door was still dead bolted on the inside, so how did she get in.

It was clear someone had gone through my papers. The papers on the table were all shoved off onto the floor and my books had been gone through. It had all been searched, yet nothing had been taken. When I left for the office that morning, I was glad to be out of that place.

Once in the office I started to review what had happened that night. That creature whether it was a woman or something else had entered my apartment somehow but not through the door. The windows are seventeen stories up, no balconies and non-opening. There had to be a means of entry and that is what I was going to concentrate on.

After the boss had come and went, I sat back in my chair and started to review my apartment in my mind. There was only one entrance from the outside and it was the front door. The windows were solid and did not open. To come through a window would require breaking it.

The walls to the adjoining apartments were eight inches thick and covered with five eights inch sheet rock and none of the sheet rock was damaged. No there had to be something else that allowed her or it to gain entry and to exit as well.

At that point I went to the restroom and did my thing. As I was turning to approach the sink, I saw a small flash in the corner of the mirror over the sink. It wasn't much, but it was enough so I saw it and knew it was there. As I walked up to the mirror, I could see nothing unusual about it. For all intent and purposes, it was a mirror. It was mounted solid to the wall and was not damaged in any way.

I finished washing my hands and then started to turn; when I got to almost a ninety-degree angle to the mirror, I saw the flash again, in the lower right-hand corner. I turned back to the mirror and looked it over from top to bottom. It was a mirror and nothing more. I then did a 90 degree turn to my left and stepped out of line with the mirror and stopped.

As I watched the mirrors lower right-hand corner, I saw it again and this time I was ready. It was almost like a small window opened. It was hard as hell to see, but it was there and I was sure of that.

Now I had something to work on. I left the restroom and returned to my office. As I walked down the hall and passed the other offices, I would look in to each office, they all had mirrors on one wall opposite the desk. When I got to my office it was the same, a mirror directly across from my desk.

I walked in and over to the windows, looking out onto the lawn and then set myself up so my peripheral vision was aligned with the mirror. When I turned toward the mirror, there it was a tiny twinkle, like a small piece of confetti was on someone's hair. When they turn the light catches it and it flashes.

The mirrors, they were the way in and out. I had no idea as to how they could do it, but I had seen that thing in my bedroom doorway and it had to have gotten into the apartment by some means.

Mirrors, we spend hours a week standing in front of them. We use them to decorate our homes and work places. We even carry them with us and use them in our cars. If you think about it, our lives are tied to mirrors in one fashion or another day in and day out.

Mirrors, but how do they come through them? From my side it is a solid. Well as solid as glass can be. It's actually a liquid from a scientific perspective. Wait, on my side it is near solid, but on their side, it could be liquefied or a gel like liquid.

They could literally swim through it. No, that doesn't make one bit of sense. It can't have one quality on one side and a totally different quality on the other side. If I pulled the mirror off the wall, it would be solid on the back side. Still, it had to be. They could hit me at any time, any place and I was defenseless.

But, how do I protect myself from them gaining entry. When I look into a mirror, I see myself in reverse. As I raise my right hand, my image in the mirror raises its left hand. It's the right to me, but from the reflections point of view it is the left. So, it raises its left hand. God, that's totally stupid and nuts. No, it's really true though.

If I hold a paper with a word on it the word will appear backward in the mirror. Now, if I take a second mirror and hold it up and view the backward word in the first mirror with the second mirror, the word appears forward or proper. So, a mirror is a reverser of one's perspective. It takes what is in my reality and turns it around. I'm accustomed to the reversed image and have learned to carry out whatever I'm doing in front of the mirror without difficulty. I've become accustomed to it. It's a way of life.

Now if someone was on the other side of the mirror looking at me and I raised my right hand, that person would see it as his left hand. When two people face one another and they both raise their right hand it is opposite for both of them. If we shake right hands, we will cross over to do that. We both remain right-handed individuals. In the mirror I appear as a left-handed individual to myself.

That was it, the mirrors. I had at least five mirrors in my apartment and two of those were full size mirrors. If they are portals then their ability to gain access to my apartment was obvious. Now I had to come up with a defense.

I could remove the mirrors and eliminate their access, but would it make me more secure. I'm sure they have alternative methods of gaining access. No, I had to have something that would stop them. That would reverse them and I knew right then and there it needed to be mirrors.

That evening on the way home from work I stopped at a furniture store and purchased five new mirrors, two of them full sized. As I took them to the car it dawned on me, I was carrying their gateway with me.

No, I could not place them in the car that would be stupid. It's the same as it would be if I were home. I will stack them facing one another. The fifth and smallest one I would place between two of the larger ones. That would protect me until I got home.

When I got home, I made sure I carried them to my apartment two at a time and facing each other. I kept the small mirror between two of the larger ones while moving it to my room. Believe me when I tell you walking across the parking lot carrying two mirrors facing one another was not easy, but all was going well. That is until one of the older ladies on my floor saw me.

They're nice old ladies, but are the nosiest people I have ever met and this one was the worst. It was Mildred and she was all I needed at that time. "You have some new mirrors, how nice. Let me see what they look like?"

I knew it, she has to know everything and pass judgment on everything, no matter what. "Please Mildred I don't have time right now to show you."

She was persistent and I had to be just as persistent back. What the hell was going on? This lady never said boo to me any other times we came across one another and here she is trying to inspect my new mirrors. The alarms went off the chart and I literally pushed her out of the way.

I opened the apartment door and stepped through setting the two mirrors against the wall next to the wall mounted mirror. I had to do this as quickly as possible. I knew they were waiting for me. I carefully arranged them to avoid giving access to me while setting them up opposite one another. I then returned to the car and got the other three mirrors and returned to the apartment and set them into place. I realized the risk I was facing while placing the last mirror in its place, but that was the only way I could do it, take the risk. I then sat down and waited.

They could have been here waiting for me or was it a situation where I had to be present before they could enter. That was an interesting thought and one I would have to address later. With the mirrors all in place and blocking their view into the room and in fact reversing their view I had no idea what it would do.

It was around three that morning when I heard the noise. It was coming from the area of the mirror by the front door. I turned and looked and the mirror on the wall was moving. Just then I saw a leg come through the mirror and start to come down on the floor when it appeared to be pulled up and into the mirror opposite the one on the wall. Like a flash the body came out of the wall mirror and went directly into the free-standing mirror.

I didn't expect the actions and reactions of the creature as it tried to enter my room and then fight to keep from being pulled into the return mirror, it was something I had not expected or anticipated.

The screams of that creature fighting

for its life will fill my mind for months and years to come, yet it was trying to come into my home and do to me what it or they had done to Beatrice.

It worked. They had tried to gain entry into my apartment again and the mirrors reversed them. But I saw it and I was glad as hell it passed on through. It was the woman again, but this time I got a better look at it and I can assure you it was not a woman, not by any stretch of the word. Oh, it had long hair, but that was about the end of the similarity. If I were to use a common term for it, I would say it looked more like a gargoyle than anything human.

Wow, my mind flashed back to Beatrice and what she must have faced when they came for her. The terror she must have felt when she realized what was happening. Here I am sitting here all alone and I can assure you I was scared silly. I can't even imagine what Beatrice felt when that thing came at her.

How far back had these creatures been watching us? How far back did mankind create the access portal for them, the mirror? If I remember right the first glass mirrors were made by the Romans in the first century.

It was not until the Middle Ages when gargoyles were first seen. Yet, there were other creatures seen back in the time of the Greeks and Egyptians. In those times they used polished metal for mirrors.

So, it appears at the time the human race was starting its meteor like growth, mirrors of some type came into existence and so they were probably starting to take control of us all the way back to that time, when man was getting into his intellectual period and the beginning of our technological growth. They started their attack on our dimension and over some seven thousand years they have come to control us for whatever purpose.

Cycles, it was all about cycles and the use of mirrors to monitor us and to view their manipulation of our cycles. How do you deal with something as old and ingrained as this? Something that has grown along with our development, something that is so much a part of us under normal conditions we see nothing and recognize nothing.

Yet, history has shown the connection between us and them. The beings have been sent into our dimension to correct and remove whatever they perceive as a danger to their status over us.

Whole social structures have been erased or altered by their presence here in our dimension, a situation in which we had no choice, and they were holding all the cards. Just how in the heck do you overcome something that is as ingrained as this thing was? Only time would tell and we didn't have much of that left.

I sat there letting all this run through my mind and looking where the creature had tried to enter my apartment and was sent back by the new mirror I had installed. It was almost overwhelming to sit there and try to comprehend what was going on. In just under a week, I had determined our social structure was totally under the control of these being and had been for several thousand years.

Chapter Five

BACK TO THE PRESENT

Needless to say, at this point I stopped thinking. I figured I could bring my findings to the Group and they could help me deal with the issue. What a bone head mistake that was. I should have known if the Cyclers were in fact controlling us, those areas of greatest importance would be the areas of our intellectual application.

These were the places where change started and was completed in our dimension and it would be these places, they would concentrate their control over us.

I had gone to see Dean Singer on the Wednesday we had set the appointment. He was a well-meaning man, but had the interest of the college way over that of Beatrice. Or, was it the interest of the Cyclers that was paramount to him or them?

Once I had introduced myself and he had seen the letter from my old job, he opened up a little. He gave me Beatrice's notebook and a number of letters she had written to a number of other scientists she tried to gain some assistance from. To the man they refused her. That would be predictable when considering who the Cyclers really put their control time into.

When we finished our meeting and as I drove back home, I thought over what he said. He was scared, I could tell from the start. It took a lot of courage for him to see me and he did his best to help, but he also knew something beyond him was going on and he needed to be extremely careful.

I don't know if he had read any of her works on cycles, but I had a fairly good feeling he knew what was going on and he was helpless against it. He was in a bad situation and I didn't help it any.

I found myself watching my rear-view cameras a little more than usual. Oh, the cameras? Yeah, I had bought a kit and replaced the mirrors in my car with rear looking cameras in order to avoid any mirrors. Strange as it sounds, it worked great. I think it's even better than mirrors as well.

So, there it was. I returned home and the next morning made the mistake of going to the boss and his board. I forgot these things were controlling us and that meant they were controlling those at the think tanks as well. Of course, they were. That was a place where major social decisions were being formulated and made. No, I blew it that time and they almost got me.

They wanted me there with all my documentation and evidence and were willing to let me retrieve everything from the apartment and bring it back to them. Thanks to Phil, he took me home and was to help me get back. Of course, he was, that was his job and it cost him his life. So, the people who had me were not Cyclers, but who they were I still did not know.

They had saved my life for sure and now I needed to learn more about them. As I looked over the infirmary room, I noted there were no mirrors or reflective surfaces. I then recalled the place was covered with cameras of every kind and size.

These people know and probably knew

a hell of a lot more than I did. My next big decision was whether I was going to cooperate with them and seek their aid or try and remain separated. Come on, I need help and I need someone who is aware of what is going on globally. These people obviously do and I need to get involved.

That afternoon, early afternoon, Mister Hammerstrong came into my room and as he sat down, he said. "Larry, I'm really sorry for what happened, but we needed to make sure we had control of you and not someone else."

He was covering his rear end and I knew it. This guy was one hell of a careful dude and I needed to get on his good side and do it fast. I looked at him. "You mean the Cyclers?"

"You, Mister Manchester are one sharp guy. First of all, please call me Reggie. Now, to address your question, that's right and you're free of them now."

The questions were screaming to be asked as I tried to formulate some order. "Larry, how much do you know about them?"

I don't know if he was following a fixed list of questions or what, but they were fitting in just great with what I had to say, "Just what I have managed to accumulate in the last three weeks. As you know, I started working for Mid Atlantic Group at the first of March. My first assignment was a paper written by Beatrice Melenkowskie. At first, I saw it as a poorly written paper and returned it to the file as unacceptable. That saved my life. But that caused me to want to know what this woman had discovered and if I could assist her in any way.

"I could not drop my analysis of her paper. Once I got into really detailed analysis of it, I found the message she left for someone, anyone, to find. After I had two clear experiences with Cyclers.

"It gained access to my apartment and I was able to determine the access point were the mirrors in my apartment. I used additional mirrors to reverse their access. I don't think it was a pleasant experience for the thing that was trying to come through.

"Yesterday, when I went in to work the hammer fell on me. I was called into the board meeting and they locked the doors and started in on me. They were trying to convince me I was crazy, insane and they were there to help me. I managed to get them to agree to let me present everything I had learned and I needed all my papers and evidence from my apartment. That is what they wanted and they agreed to send Phil to transport me.

"Hell, I should have known. He had mirrors in his car and they were on top of me like they owned me. I saw the car following us and thought nothing of it. It wasn't until I was in the apartment, I knew I was in real trouble. At the time I thought the Cyclers were responsible for the mayhem in that apartment, but I now know it was you."

Reggie started to nod his head as I spoke and when I finished, he looked at me, "Larry, I'm sorry for that, but we were moving as fast as we could. They tried to gain entry two times while my people were there, but your mirror defense worked great, thank you."

I could tell he was being honest with me, but I was still angry over the way they took me, "I understand now sir, but at the time I was scared to death. My only question now sir, is where do we go from here? I mean, will I be able to pursue this issue while I'm here?

By this time, he was in deep thought and was surely weighing the odds in regards to letting me pursue this issue, "That Larry is the sixty-four-million-dollar question. Perhaps we need to sit down with the rest of my lead team and talk this whole thing over."

That was better than I had anticipated and I went along with him. "That sir, I am most willing to do."

That appeared to be the end of the conversation for all intent and purposes, "All right, let's plan it for tomorrow morning in the main lounge. If you want, we can transfer you to another apartment that is better suited for you."

I was sure I was being monitored here in this place and in the new location I would be taken to. I decided to stay put and not change things too much at this time. Kind of a defense thing I guess, but it felt better that way, "No, not right now. This will do me just fine until the meeting. After that we can decide."

The fact was I did not what to change anything. I knew where the cameras were in this room and I felt sure I could work around them. I had all of their surveillance equipment located and I knew there were a couple of black areas in the room and decided I could use them.

Mister Hammerstrong stood up and

started to leave and then turned back to me. He had a concerned expression on his face, "You still don't trust us do you Larry?"

I looked in his eyes. He was truly an earnest man, trying to do the right thing. "Sir, right now I would say I halfway trust you, but after the last few days I find it difficult to trust anyone."

He was nodding his head and raised his right hand almost in surrender and turned to leave, "Larry, I understand, in the morning Larry, in the morning."

When he got to the door, I noticed he hesitated. He then turned and walked back to me and sat down. "Larry, I need to talk to you about something else right now and it's important."

Twenty minutes later he got up and opened the door and left. I couldn't help but wonder how all this was going to turn out.

After he left, I laid back and started to think again. How long had this battle, this war been going on? When did people finally discover they were being manipulated by these things, these Cyclers? In the end, what could we, or anyone, do about it?

So far all I've been able to do is come up with an endless list of questions. Yes, I had made several discoveries, but still the questions clearly outnumbered the achievements. I was beginning to think there was going to be no end to this process.

Not knowing what was on the other side of the mirrors. We had no idea as to how formidable they were. Could they control the world by force, could they destroy the world if they desired? Not knowing hardly anything about your enemy is worse than knowing.

How big an organization are they? How vast are their numbers? If they had the technology to control us, what technology did they have to fight us with? I was starting to get mad as hell over this situation. The longer it went on the more I was determined to figure it out, one way or the other.

Gees, this was impossible. Just then it came on me. Is it possible for us to view them, to watch them, to see what they are and what they have? Surely if they can see us and transport themselves between their world and ours, then the reverse should be true.

That was an intriguing idea and one we would have to explore. That fit in well with my feeling that to know my enemy was more important than being able to fight him. The knowledge will tell me how to fight and that is a winning combination.

My next concern involved their environment compared to ours. It appears they can survive in our environment, but is the same true for us? That is assuming we can enter their world by some means.

Their environment may be harsher than ours and so it is an easy switch over for them. Again, knowing them would determine if we can invade and what equipment we may need to make that move against them.

It was then a plan started to build in my mind. We need to capture one of them and figure out just what it is we are dealing with. But, how do we do that? Mirrors! Bring in a mirror and place it in a controlled environment and then when one enters through the mirror, we have it.

Sounds easy, but it's not. We may have it, but then what do we do? It's like grabbing the tail of a Tiger. Once you have a hold of it, you dare not let go, but on the other hand keeping a hold on its tail makes you an easy target for it claws.

To bring a mirror into this facility would be dangerous, yet I think it can be done. What if we took two mirrors and placed them one facing the other while we shipped them here? We keep them in that orientation until we are ready and then separate them and leave one open to the area, we want the creature in.

Good idea, but it's too simplistic. There is a lot of engineering that needs to go into building a double mirror system that will permit entry into our space and then keep the target after it enters.

Wait a minute that made me think, they were in a different world? I've been saying that for some time now and it's an assumption I should not have made. First, I need to define the term world. When I say that word it brings up a mental view of a planet spinning in space. Who said they came from space? No, I'm wrong there. It is not another world, it's another dimension.

These creatures are right next door. Their entire universe is sitting just on the other side of that mirror. If these creatures are from another dimension, then could they be controlling other dimensions besides ours as well?

How far out do these things reach and influence other systems? What a nightmare! This is as close to being impossible as anything I could think up on my own.

All right, where am I? We have a society of beings who have discovered a way to travel between dimensions. They do this for some specific reason, what that is I do not know as yet.

Right now, that is the best guess as to where they come from. If they were of this dimension then there would be sightings of all kinds among those who are opposed to them and have managed to get out from under their control.

They control their neighboring dimensions through the biological cycles of those species in the dimensions they have infiltrated. But what are the reasons, why, and how are they benefiting in this process? That question is the key to everything and that is the issue we have to figure out. There has to be a reason for them doing this. There must be a benefit to them, but what?

I don't know how long I worked on this. All I know is sometime during the evening, I guess, a young woman brought me my meal. After that my mind went into over drive and I was back at it again.

Somewhere along the way, while working on this puzzle, I passed out from exhaustion. I have no idea what time it was when she woke me up, but I felt refreshed and ready to take this thing on. I had a plan and I meant to introduce it to this group of people at the coming meeting.

My attendant returned to remind me of the meeting time. She showed me the facilities, left me a complete set of clothing and then left. I found everything I needed there, but no mirrors. What a neat idea. They had a monitor with a camera attached to it and I used that as my mirror.

After the shower she returned and took me to the dining hall. Mister Hammerstrong got up and came to greet me. For the first time I took a good look at him. He was a big man. Had to be at least six feet five inches at a minimum. He must have weighed in at around two hundred and forty plus pounds. I had no doubts he was a powerful man as well.

Up to this point I had been involved in a mystery that at first had little or no rational to it. I had stumbled onto something that was so crazy and dangerous I had been neutralized and unable to assert myself in my dealing with it. I was now going to take the step and see just how far I could go and how dedicated these people were to their cause, if they had one.

We sat down and had a good breakfast spending most of our time in small talk. This was beginning to build our relationship to one another and we both could feel it. They had started this whole thing by bringing me here and now I was going to get some answers and I was going to get them now. "What do you think of our little fortress anyway?" He asked.

Having seen only a limited part of the facilities I had no basis to make a judgment from. "I believe I have never seen anything like it before. How long have you been building it?"

Reggie was up to the little digging game. "Our society started building this place about fifty years ago, just after they discovered the Cyclers."

That was impressive. Fifty years was a long time for any group of people to build something as impressive as this and still remain hidden. "How long have you been here?"

Reggie pointed at himself. "Larry, I believe I have been here most of my life. Actually, I've been here about twenty-five years now."

Again, I was impressed. He actually did not look that old, "Twenty-five years here, inside this place?"

Reggie smiled and sat back looking at me. "No, I've been out working special details from time to time, but the better part of my time has been in here.

"This is actually one of a dozen such facilities spread out across the whole of the world. We make up a fairly large army."

I sat there listening to what he said and it all sounds great except for one thing. This social order had been going for fifty years and they still were sitting here doing whatever it was they were doing and really not doing much. "Are you ready to do anything about this problem?"

The smile slowly slid from his face and then he got thoughtful, "Yes we are, and we plan to start our move within the next year."

I watched as he spoke and listen closely to him. He was not too sure of himself on that subject and was also somewhat uncomfortable. Hell, this thing is more of a game than an actual attempt to deal with this problem and that was assuming they even knew if there was a problem. All right, what he said sounded fine, but the big question was. "Can you beat them?"

Reggie sat up and brought his hands up

to the jaw and then leaned toward me. "Well, we're sure going to try. But our problem is we don't know who we're fighting. I mean, we know about the Cyclers and their control over the human race.

"What we don't know are the important things about them, their appearance, their size, their numbers, and their technology. Obviously, their technology is rather advanced, but their ability to go to war is still a question. No, we need more intelligence about them and until we get that any attempt to go to war with them is sure to fail."

I sat there looking at him, "Mister Hammerstrong,"

"Larry, please this would be much more comfortable is you would call me Reggie."

I smiled as I watched him squirm and readjust his position in his chair. This man knew they were doing nothing and he seemed to be at a loss as to what he or they should be doing. I needed to watch him closely so I continued. "All right, Reggie, where do you feel these beings come from?"

Evidently that was a good question because it seemed to push a button and he was off. "Larry, we are sure they are dimensional beings. That is, they come from a different dimension than ours, the makeup of which we do not know as yet. We know they can enter and function in our dimension, but we do not know if the same is true for us."

They were on it, but they did not appear to be pursuing it as hard as I felt they should be. I looked around the mess area and could see the people there appeared to be in good condition and well fed.

If that was right then I would think they would be working hard at making their next move, but they weren't. "Yes, I've come to the same conclusion. I know by the gargoyles physical build; its environment has to be gravitationally much stronger than ours. They are built low and powerfully.

"I have a feeling we would not fare well on their side. By the size of the gargoyle's ears, sound does not travel well on their side. That would speak to a heavy atmosphere and probably high humidity.

"Have you considered trying to capture one of those things, whatever they are?"

Reggie hands dropped to the table top and he sat back. "Yes, we have and as yet we have not been able to do it. They're fast and their smart and when in our dimension they seem to be able to move much faster and quicker than we can. It may be because of the differences in our environment that makes it easier for them to move."

Damn, this man looked to be a person capable of doing whatever he wanted to do and do it well. The problem was he had been here so long he and everyone else in this place was comfortable with the status quo and as a result nothing was happening.

My mind was starting to roll at this time. "I think you're probably right there. If that is the case then we are not going to be able to function in their dimension."

Reggie nodded his head. "Yes, we came to the same conclusion."

I then had an idea and started into it. I needed to get into this thing and find out just what this place was capable of and if it was possible to get their leadership to start leading. "Reggie, what I would like to see is one of these things in our hands and under our control. But, that's not all. I would love to be able to wire one of them up and send them back to see if we can get a visual of their side and maybe some insight as to what we need to do and how to go about it."

Reggie was perking up now. I don't know if he actually was interested or was just leading me along. Anyway, I decided to keep going. "Larry, that's an idea no one has thought of before?"

I looked at Reggie and shrugged my shoulders. To be totally honest with you I would have expected much more from a facility like this and yet nothing is going on. "Reggie, if you were to pursue a capture of one of these things how would you do it?"

He sat there looking at me and looked around the dining room and then back to me. He started to say something and then withdrew and just sat there. "We haven't, because of the speed of these things. It just hasn't worked itself out."

I couldn't believe his answer. It was weak and frankly a bunch of crap. "Wait a minute. You're telling me your society has been around for fifty years and during all that time and with several bases all across the world no one has ever thought of capturing one of the gargoyles while they were in our dimension?"

He sat there looking at me like I had caught him in a compromising position. "No, I did not mean it that way. There have been suggestions we should try and capture them and we did attempt, but once in our dimension they are fast and we have yet to catch them off guard.

"Larry, I guess I was jumping the gun here and made an assumption you wanted to attack their dimension and capture one that way. And, I know that's not what you said, but it is a touchy point for us and as yet we have failed miserably in trying to capture one or anything from their side."

Now was the time to see if this guy was real or just pulling me along. "Well Reggie, the first thing we need to do is get one. Once we have it, we can do whatever we want in trying to communicate with it. Whatever we do, when that is done, I want to kill it and then bug it and send it back.

"They're going to receive it and conduct their own studies as to how and by what mean it died. While they're doing that, we will be pulling our data back to our side and getting a good look at them and their environment.

"Reggie, we need intelligence about their side and their capabilities before we can do anything else. Nothing is more important at this time than intelligence. We have to have it."

This time Reggie appeared to be really

interested and he was starting to think. "That's one hell of a plan Larry. The one thing that concerns me is how we keep the communications link going between their dimension and ours. That will be a tough nut to crack."

I had thought of that before and I had an idea. "I don't think so Reggie. I would bet we have all the equipment and hardware we need right here on this base to do just that.

"We will need to install video and sound capabilities in the body. We can hide them in the eyes and ears of the creature and they should be fairly safe for a period of time before they are discovered. As we send the body back through the mirror, we attach a hair antenna to the body and break it off once it is back across into their dimension. With that we will have the hair antenna hanging through the mirror and receiving the signals from the implants in the body."

Reggie started to shake his head while I was finishing my sentence. "It will never work. They will discover the signals and the antenna almost as soon as they see the body."

I was ready for that one as well. "That they may do, but we will still get a glimpse of them and their dimension and that will be worth everything. For us it will be the first time they have been made vulnerable and it is worth everything. For the first time they will be on the receiving end of the game and that can have a far reaching impact on this whole game."

Reggie slapped the table top. "Larry, you are one devious son-of-a-gun and I think I love you for it. Let's get to the meeting and start to work this up. We'll need to throw all our resource at this task and do everything possible to make it succeed. Damn, it's been a long time since I've felt this energized."

As the group started to gather, Reggie introduced me to each one as they came in. Most were around my age and seemed to be well educated and committed to this facility. Once everyone had arrived Reggie started the program by giving everyone a briefing as to how we got to this point. He made it short and to the point, after all there was not much to discuss.

Finally, he introduced me and advised those present to listen closely to what I had to say. Now was my chance to clear the air and finally tell someone, somebody what I knew and what I thought was going on.

I walked them through the Beatrice'

Milankovitch Paper and what it had revealed to me. I advised them I thought Beatrice was dead and had been taken by the Cyclers to be sure she no longer would pursue her discovery.

I went over the message and then the visit by the gargoyle at my apartment. I covered how I had secured the apartment from further entry and then moved on into my perception of who these beings were and what we should or could do about it.

Finally, it was time for the major part of my presentation and it was going to be a doozy. At this point I was totally into my presentation. I was hiding nothing. As I watched their faces, I knew I was making an impact. I only hoped I was not blowing it.

The thought crossed my mind I had only been in this place three days and now I was standing in front of this group and laying it all out for them and getting ready to move into a leadership role and start to tell them what they were going to do and when they were going to do it. That in itself was crazy to the limit. This was the moment when all hell would break out or they would fall into place and go with it.

I started the final part of my

presentation. "Three days ago, I was unceremoniously brought into this facility. At the time I was scared to death and did not really know who you were or what you were up to. After my situation in the interrogation room, I ended up in the infirmary, and for two days I was able to really think this over and I have come up with what I think are some novel ideas and methods of addressing the Cyclers.

"While in the infirmary I got to wondering how and when the Cyclers came in touch with mankind and how they came to control us. We now know they have gained access to us through mirrors. If we go back in history, we will see at the time men started having contacts with strange and terrifying creature was at about the time we started to use reflective devices as mirrors. Obviously, you know this because there are no mirrors in this base that I have seen.

"The Egyptians and Greeks used polished metals for their mirrors. It was not until the Roman Empire when the first of the glass mirrors came into existence. At that time the increase in direct person to creature events began to take place.

"From the time of the Egyptians and

Greeks to the Romans the Cyclers spent time studying their new subjects. They watched our biological cycles and developed ways and means of influencing them.

Over on the other side of the world the Chinese and Japanese were advancing and they too fell under the control of the Cyclers through mirrors, probably before those in Europe and the Middle East.

Mankind has always been a violent creature, but over time the Cyclers developed an understanding of the cycles of power and control that let them work their way into the human biological process.

"In the process they studied our reproductive systems and the nature in which we paired up for the purpose of procreation of the species.

"They spent centuries building up their knowledge and methods of dominating us from within our cycles. Given enough time I'm sure we could find there are cycles in the times of war from the beginning of the glass mirror to today.

"I am sure we would find increases in the numbers of human males being born at times just before a major worldwide conflict, whether it was the world of the Mediterranean or global wide. The tendency for violence and the drive to power and control were manipulated by the Cyclers and the history of mankind was directed by them.

"At times when cultures were developing or making great strides, we find war breaking out and those cultures have been damaged or destroyed in order to stop or redirect their achievements. The world wars of the 20th century are a good example of destruction and redirection of our social structures.

"Even the infusions of a worldwide epidemic have been manipulated by them. The black plague in or around the 16th century was probably started and manipulated by them. The whole of Europe was decimated by that plague it would set all of Europe back for centuries. This event set us up for control and they built them in slowly and deliberately.

"If we go back in our history and trace the movement of mankind across the world and all the great achievements we have made and the great downfalls we have been subjected to, then we can be assured they have been involved.

"I guess the real question is this, has it been a benefit to mankind, or a curse? From my perspective it has been a curse. So much of the tragedy of mankind can be traced directly to our biological cycles.

"I'm sure if one of them were standing here right now it would be telling you without them, we would never have advanced to the level we're at today. I'm sure their rational clearly sees them as a benefit to us, not a burden.

"Yet, at no time did I see or hear, throughout history, if mankind was asked or invited to voice our acceptance or rejection of their interference in our growth. The question I would have been how much of our growth has been stymied by them? If they had not interfered in our world, where would we be today? Let your imagination deal with that.

"I am a Homosapien. I have my own intelligence and I wish to be the master of my own destiny. To even so much as believe I am under the control of another being is repulsive to me.

"My life is a series of cycles in every conceivable area or process of life and it must not be a tool of my control. I retain my right to be as I wish to be and not to be what some creature in another dimension determines I should be, even unto my destruction.

"It has taken us around seven thousand years to come to the realization these beings are a fact and they have control over our lives and our development. It leads me to the conclusion the beings you control, in time, will become as intelligent as you who control them. When that time comes, the controlled will rebel and the controller will pay the price for their arrogance and shortsightedness.

"So, here we are today and we are in a position where we can do something about those who have dominated us. I have developed a plan over the last two days. The fact is it has been brewing in me for some time. And it is now we need to move.

"In order to really know our enemy, we must learn all we can of them, both mentally and physically. With that I propose we initiate a plan to capture one of our tormentors. What I offer you is the shell of a plan and it will need to be perfected in detail before we venture to do it.

"My proposal is to use the mirror as the tool of their capture. We know they view, control, and initiate contact with us through the mirror. History has shown they have had direct and intense contact with humanity in the past. The number and types of creatures that have come to this world to contact many among us has been recorded over time.

"I saw and managed to survive a direct contact with one. At first, I thought it was a woman. It appeared to be around four feet tall and proportioned to that size body frame. I was looking at it in silhouette and did not get a good, in color view, of the overall creature. The way it moved and the way it reacted told me this creature was powerful and something I did not want to have a hand-to-hand contact with.

"That happened while I was in bed in my apartment one night at around three or four in the morning. The way the door to my bedroom opened into the room controlled how the light from my hallway entered the room. That left me in the dark and I had the fortitude to remain quiet and not move. It stepped further into the room and still could not see me. I would later determine this thing was in fact a gargoyle.

"It finally left after about thirty seconds and left the apartment. After that event I looked my apartment over. At the time, I thought it had come into the apartment through the front door. When I looked, I found nothing violated in the least bit.

"It was the following day while at work I went into the restroom and just as I was leaving, I caught a small flash out of the lower right-hand corner of the mirror. I turned and looked and then started to turn away again and I saw the flash a second time. I left the restroom and as I was going home that evening, I determined it was the mirrors.

"On the way home, I stopped at a furniture store and bought several mirrors and took them home. My reasoning was if they entered my apartment through the mirrors, then the mirrors would be my weapon against them. This proved to be the perfect defense against these creatures.

"There was a problem at this point. If they entered our world through the mirrors, then my taking five mirrors into my vehicle was inviting trouble. So, I turned the mirrors facing one another and then wrapped them with heavy paper. I also taped paper across my vehicle mirrors as well. I knew enough that I had to eliminate any direct access into my car.

"So, using the same rational when I got home, I would use the mirrors as a defense. If they came through the mirror, I reasoned they could be sent back by the mirror. So, I set a mirror up facing each and every mirror in my apartment. After doing that my second experience happened with the gargoyle that night.

"I decided to stay up that evening and at around three in the morning I heard it coming in, it was using the large mirror by the front door as its primary point of entry. That was reasonable in that it matched its body size and would be much easier to enter through.

"I looked over at the mirror and actually saw it coming out of the mirror on the wall. This time I saw its face and it was a gargoyle for sure. It looked just like those you see on the churches across Europe. But, this time, as it entered the room it was pulled into the facing mirror.

"Now remember, when you look into a mirror it is the reverse of you. Your right hand looks to be on the left in the mirror. If you wave your right hand the image waves its left hand. The key is it is a reverse image. It reverses that which is looking into it and this is what it did to the gargoyle. It reversed and took the gargoyle back into the mirror.

"The shock of seeing it was extreme. I literally threw up on myself. If you had seen it, you would have known why. It was not a pleasant thing to see. There had to be a lot of pain in that it screamed like nothing I had ever heard before. It tried not to be drawn into the mirror and it was literally torn apart right there before my eyes.

"Immediately all the activity in the mirror stopped. You could see the surface of the mirror go solid and it stayed that way. I don't know if they had ever experienced that before, or if it is an event they experienced before but so rare it was like a new experience to them.

"With that my plan is to use the mirror to capture one of them and if all works well, we will be able to then use the creature as the transporter of a video and audio system it will take back into its own dimension.

"I plan on using a hair antenna that would pass from this dimension into theirs and then capture anything and everything that comes back to us. I would expect we would only get a few minutes of video and audio before they find the equipment and kill it. But that may well be just enough for us.

"The mirror system would be made up of two three by six-foot-high quality mirrors. I would suggest they be made of a thick strong bullet resistant glass. The two mirrors would be made facing one another and transported in that way as well.

"We would mount them into a framework that held one mirror solidly in place and the other one set up on a movable track that would let it slide from the side back over the mirror on the solid mount. That way we can open the portal, so to speak, and let a creature in, and then we, not them, can close the portal and lock the creature into our capture room.

"I propose this system be set up in a room that is made of solid walls, at least three feet thick. No windows at all. If we want to see into the room then we use video. The door will be a solid steel door no less than a foot thick and with a vault style locking system.

"Once a creature enters the room the movable mirror will slide back into place solid against the solid mounted mirror with a locking system that locks the two mirrors together. That will put the creature in the room and under our complete control. The only thing we need do at the time is to immobilize it."

Just then a hand went up in the middle of the room and that person asked. "How do we do that?"

148

I nodded in understanding and shrugged my shoulders. "That my friends we will figure out once we have it."

A second person over to my right asked. "What if we kill it?"

"Well, if we want a live one to study then we have a problem. If we kill it, we try again. We will eventually kill it once we've had a chance to study it to some degree. Once we are done then we kill it and prepare it for re-insurgence back into its dimension along with our camera and audio systems.

"I have a strong feeling they will keep feeding gargoyles through that mirror until they achieve whatever it is, they want to achieve. I think they are limited in what they can actually see in any one place and so their picture of us is rather choppy, but it's enough to control us.

"Well, that's the fundamentals of my plan. It has a lot of work that still needs to be done, but I guess the real question is will it work? That is what you must determine. How say you?"

I sat down and Reggie stood up and asked everyone for input. One young man stood up, started to walk away from his seat, then stopped and turned around. "I don't know if he is nuts or just plain crazy. The idea we bring a mirror into this facility is without a doubt so stupid I find it hard to even comment about.

"Second, to think we could control, let alone implant any devices on these creatures is beyond me. As far as I'm concerned you can take your plan and shove it."

His reaction hit me funny. I wanted to get up and go over and slap him silly. Instead, I stood and looked him in the face. "Look, I did not say this was the way we must go. I said this is a plan I have developed. The thing I see, and apparently, you're incapable of seeing, is that we need to do something.

"You have an organization here. What is it for? Are you here simply to confirm the actions of these Cyclers? Or are you here to try and come up with a way and means of overcoming their control over the human race?

"If neither one of these issues are what you're here for, then you must be here for nothing and are content to live this kind of life. I think it's time you either do something or shut this place down."

He stood there looking at me. It was clear he was panicking and his fear of the

Cyclers was more than his willingness to challenge them. I noticed his hands were shaking and I looked over at Reggie. He nodded his head and I sat down and two others stood and walked over to the young man and took him out of the meeting.

Just then a young woman stood. "He's been fighting this thing for five years now. Just after his father and mother came up missing. We determined they had become victims of the Cyclers. He means well, but carries a lot of fear with him."

I did not know this woman, but her compassion for this young man was obvious. "I understand. I've had the same feeling, but that does not deal with the problem. It's still there and will never go away until we put it away."

"Look, I'm new here, but I'm also well versed in Cyclers and their impact on us. I was completely overcome with fear and depression when I discovered these beings. But that passed fast and I then started to figure out how to beat them and set us free.

"Right now, our biggest handicap is the lack of information and knowledge about these things. We need to get as much information on them as we can pull together.

That is going to be the only way we can deal with them and bring their domination over us to an end.

"I am a newcomer here, but right now I believe I have a greater understanding and knowledge base than any of you here about this whole Cyclers situation. Without knowing I was on the verge of this discovery; I had spent years studying cycles of every conceivable kind. The entirety of the universe functions on cycles. Sit back and take a look at it and you will come to understand. Everything is cyclical.

"Look, consider the animal kingdom. Each and every animal, lives by a set of cyclical rules. Year in and year out they cycle through everything they do. We call is instinct, but it is in fact cycles. The difference between animals and humans is the intellect of the human race. That has been the single greatest obstacle to our being fully controlled and dominated by the Cyclers.

"But they, the Cyclers, keep working on it and, in time, they will gain complete domination over the human race. Let's go back in history a short distance. In the 20th century, I would say around 1970 or there about, we will find a social phenomenon take place across the world. A social change came in and through this social change the human race became closer to the animal world than it has ever been before.

"There were huge changes in our attitude toward immoral and unethical lifestyles. Whole social structures were torn apart from within. Drugs became a huge involvement in this change and then it went right into the sexual standards of the most advanced societies on the planet.

"Along with that came the age of the terrorists and means of trying to control their fellow humans became the one and only purpose to the many varied radical elements across the world.

"Government and national stability suffered terribly during that time. The movement to electronic gadgetry shifted into full force and the control of the social order fell into the so-called internet and the other related communications systems. Whole sections of the social structure started losing their social skills and people began to be isolated.

"No one thought anything about how these sudden changes came about. The so-called experts simply marked it up to being internal social changes were inevitable. To put it in a simple term, the world went crazy. And, so here we are today. Their total domination of us is the closest it has ever been, and if we do not act, we will in fact become the animals they desire us to be.

"I have no idea as to why they do this or even want to. There is nothing physical they can gain from it, absolutely nothing. They can only access us through the mirrors and so there must be something else that drives them and I believe it is the sense of power, the control of another race or dimension.

"I believe we are not the only dimension they have been trying to control or are controlling. No, we are in a position where we must act soon or we will never again have the opportunity or ability to resist them."

Everyone sat there. No one said a word, yet you could feel the sense of agreement running through those present. Finally, the heads started nodding and Reggie stood.

"Ladies and gentlemen, it appears Larry here has touched our consciousness and we are now beginning to realize we have spent a lot of time getting ready and no time moving ahead.

"We have the technology and the people needed to take the next step. I guess what we needed was for someone to come along and jerk our chain and get us moving again. It's time to decide."

Chapter Six

TIME TO FIGHT BACK

I had been given the opportunity to have my say about our current situation and how I felt about this overall issue. If nothing else, I was able to clear my inner being. At that point Reggie stepped up to the front. "All right, are there any more objections to Larry's thoughts and preliminary plans?"

We looked around the group and no one had any objections. With that Reggie started the process of brain storming the methods and means we would follow to achieve our goal.

Within an hour we had a list of objectives and targets we could work on. He set up groups to address each and every issue and then to bring their findings back to the main meeting later on that afternoon.

I returned to my room and sat down to

go over what I had said and reported earlier. There was something I had missed and I knew it, but just what it was I could not bring up. I have learned in the past if I simply play the past hours back to myself often enough, I would find the problem. My gut feeling told me there was something more to the outburst the young man had made. My sense was he was trying to tell me something.

As I started that process it occurred to me the issue was not what I had said, but the response of the young man. One thing was sure, he was scared, but what was he scared of? I assumed it had been the Cyclers, but maybe just maybe I was wrong.

My mind went back to the exchange and what I had said just before he reacted. What was he doing at that time? What was it I failed to see he had been doing? I sat there and visualized the entirety of the room and everyone in it. What was common and uncommon about them?

Each person had a laptop computer at their place. Each had a drink and some had a snack at their place. There were pencils and tablets lying all over the desk or table tops. What was missing?

I thought about the tables again and

each place. As I did, I noted the main table at the front of the room where the leaders were sitting. Each of them had a laptop and the same items as the rest in the room. All that is, except me. I did not have a laptop. As a matter of fact, I was in a position where I could not see the screen of anyone's laptop.

My mind then went back to the young man and his actions. I assumed he was scared and his fear was the Cyclers. What did he say, 'I don't know if what you proposed was stupid or crazy' and the bringing of a mirror into the facilities was questioned? I sat there and let that race through my mind several time before it jelled.

Aw crap! Damn, they had me. Now it hit and I knew I was in real trouble. The young man was trying to warn me. He was trying to tell me something and I missed it. I let my emotions overcome me and I failed to see what he was saying. Now it was obvious.

He had stood up and moved out of the view of the laptops. Where he was standing was clear of any direct view of any of the laptop screens. Damn, I missed that completely. They did a switcheroo on me and I fell for it.

They first of all got me in a room and

put the pressure on me to the point I collapsed. Then they apologized and took me in as one of them, then the show. You ever have that feeling when you discover something is really important, but you had missed it time and again. This cold sweat comes over you and you feel your head go light. That was me right now.

Mirrors, mirrors are the portals, but the current methodology of observing was the electronics; computers, cameras and sound systems. They had us completely wired and could track us anywhere they wanted.

No mirrors, but cameras everywhere of every kind and size. That means I am being monitored right now here in this room. They have been monitoring me all along and I failed to figure it out. I knew the cameras were there, that was obvious. My problem was I failed to tie the cameras to the right point of interest, the Cyclers.

One thing I knew, I had at least two friends in this place. How do I know that? They told me so. The young man and woman are with me. Their demeanor and actions told me they were playing a balancing act and I had someone I could work with.

I decided to play along with the whole

thing. I knew now the planning game was being carried out as a means of gleaning more insight into the ways and means of dealing with us. My mirror trick had secured my life for the time being. They wanted more information on that.

The next thing I needed to do was make contact with one or both of my possible benefactors. They may know others who are opposed to what is going on here and if we can get them coordinated there may be a chance of getting through this thing alive.

The following morning, I went to breakfast and saw Reggie. I had decided I would not change my focus in regards to working with Reggie and his people, but I also needed to make contact with the two from the meeting. I walked over to where Reggie was sitting and asked where the young man who had the problem yesterday was and he pointed him out.

I needed to contact him somehow, so I decided to take the apology method. "Reggie, I need to let that young man know I hold no hard feeling against him. If it is all right for me to do that, I will go over and see him."

Reggie appeared to have little if any concern about my contacting him. He paused and then agreed and thanked me for being so kind to him.

I walked over to the table where the young man was sitting and sat down across the table from him. He looked around to see who was close by and I then asked him his name. He told me his name was Mark Manner.

I continued to address him. "Well Mark, I want you to know I have no hard feeling toward you in regards to what you said. In fact, I agree with you."

He looked at me again and then around the room. Reggie was over at his table and was watching us.

He appeared to still be nervous and could not sit still and talk to me. "Mister Manchester, do you really understand what is going on around here?"

That got my attention. "Mark, I really do. I may be new here, but I can see and I can determine what is taking place."

He sat there looking at me and listening to what I was saying. "Do you know your life is about as worthless as that dead fly there on the table?"

I have to admit I was getting a little irritated. "Right now, I do, but I think you and

I and that young woman can correct that problem if we can work together."

He pushed his plate away from him and leaned back in his chair. "That is going to be one hell of a problem. Every camera in this place is tied directly to the Cyclers and they never miss anything. In fact, the fact you and I are talking for so long, will bring about a close check on us in about two minutes."

We sat there a minute and then I saw two men walking toward us. I reached out with my hand to shake his and started talking. "Well Mark, you keep on the edge and speak as you feel you need to. I have no problem with that. If I said or did anything that causes you a problem then I am sincerely sorry."

As I spoke the two men heard me and slowed their pace down and as I stood up, they stopped and turned and went the other way.

I leaned over the table and asked. "Mark, I need to meet that young lady. What's her name?"

He was still looking around at everyone in the room. "It's Tammy Lake. She's been here around three years now and she has been working night and day trying to figure a way for us to get out of here."

Yes, that was the girl that stood up for Mark during the meeting. "All right, I'll contact her and get back to you later. Relax and let me get this thing rolling. I have nothing to lose because I'm not supposed to leave this place alive anyway."

Mark seemed to relax a bit and semi-smiled at me as I started to leave. "All right Larry, let me know when and if I can do anything for you."

I turned and walked back over to Reggie. I was taking the old Mafia adage of keeping your friends close and your enemies closer. I sat down across the table from him and leaned forward.

"Boy Reggie, that kid is scared silly. I don't know what about, but he sure as hell doesn't trust anyone here. He seems like a good man. Reggie, I think we'll get along just fine."

Reggie sat there looking at me. There was something about him I had just noticed and it was a puzzle to me. What was he thinking about? "Thanks Larry, I'm sure he was just scared. This whole thing is nothing but scary."

It was later that afternoon when I reached into my jacket pocket and found a note in there. I have no idea as to when or where it was placed there, but it turned out to be important. The note simply said. "Meet me in the game room at four o'clock, across from the main meeting room. Tammy."

I left my room and walked down the hall toward the main meeting room. I was noting all the cameras, they had this place covered. There was little if anything you could do without being directly viewed by whoever was manning those cameras.

I got to the game room door and opened it and walked in. Almost all the lights in the room were out except for a light in a vending machine at the far end of the room against the wall. I heard her voice from the far corner, "Larry, over here."

I walked back to the area and then saw her sitting at the table in the corner of the room. "Tammy?"

The area of the table was in the dark but I could see her silhouette. "Yes, please sit down. This is one of the few places in this complex where we can meet and not be monitored."

I looked around. "Why is that?
There is a camera right over there looking at us."

She half ways giggled when I said that. "No, it's not. Right now, it's looking at a playback of this spot and we have fifteen minutes to complete our business and clear out of here."

"Fifteen minutes? That's hardly enough time to get to know each other. Anyway, don't they have monitors outside who would have recorded your coming in here?"

Again, she giggled, almost like a little kid that was pulling a fast one on her mother and father. "Yes, they do and they recorded you coming into the room, but not me."

I was confused and getting more and more curious every second. "How is that?"

She looked up at the ceiling and then at me. "I came by a different means."

When she said that I froze, she sensed that. "Relax Larry, it's all right. I'm not from the Cyclers and you would learn that shortly. Over time we have been able to create a number of hidden doors throughout the facility so we can move around without being seen. This is one of the rooms we have built our passage ways into."

That immediately brought up a thought. She had said "we" and that means to me there were more than her and Mark. "How many are there of you?"

She looked right at me. "Right now, Larry, I cannot tell you that. We are not totally sure you are not one of them."

I could understand their being cautious. "I understand. But, how are you going to determine that?"

She sat there looking at me and then reached out. "Give me your hand."

Hell, I didn't know what she was up to and I asked her, "Which one?"

She reached over and grabbed my hand and pulled toward her, "Your left hand."

As I gave my left hand over to her, I laid it on the table and she reached out and took a hold of it. I saw her other hand come up from under the table with a tube-like object about four inches long and about an eighth of an inch in diameter.

The end pointing toward me was beveled and sharp. She pressed it against the meaty part of my hand and pushed. The tube entered my hand and stung like crazy. I started to pull away when a second hand came down on mine from my left and from the shadows.

I thought for sure I had just been killed, that the Cyclers had successfully killed me.

"What the hell."

I looked up and there was Mark. "Relax Larry, it's a probe and it will be helping us ensure you are who you say you are."

I knew it was Mark, but it was not registering right then. "Who the hell are you?"

He leaned over and looked me in the face. "Larry, I'm Mark."

Au shit, he scared the hell out of me and I could hardly focus on him. "What the hell, I walked into a trap."

Mark was still holding my arm and was now down on his knees beside me trying to get me to focus on him and see it was actually him. "No, you didn't.

We are a part of an internal resistance organization here at the base. This base was built and is run by the Cyclers and each of us were recruited and brought to this base to fulfill the wants and demands of the Cyclers in this region of the Earth. It has taken us almost forty years to get this far and we are extremely careful with anyone and everyone we meet."

I was starting to calm down. The hand still hurt like heck, but my mind was slowing down and I was starting to think again. "Is everyone on this base part of the resistance?"

Mark was now moving into a chair by me. "No, about two thirds are still under the control of the Cyclers and the rest of us are free of their control. We submit to them voluntary in order to prepare to resist them by force. You are our new weapon we plan to introduce to them in time."

I was still not sure of what was going on but when he said weapon that caused me to focus even that much more. "What do you mean weapon?"

Mark looked over at the door and then leaned toward me. "Larry, you have a good knowledge and understanding as to what is going on worldwide with the Cyclers. Your experiences with them have shown tremendous initiative and skills we must have to progress any further. That was why we targeted you and caused you to be brought here. What we are playing here is an eight-level chess game and so far, we are doing quite well.

"In about five days we will be taking this base. At that time, we will have control over all the monitoring tools that are spread out all over this facility. When we do, the Cyclers will do everything they can to retake this place. We will be in the fight of our lives and there will be no alternatives. We either win or we die, it's that simple. The question now is this, are you with us?"

I sat there looking at the two of them. I had completely forgotten about the tracking seed that had been implanted in my hand. This thing had just gone from nuts to totally insane. I was still not sure who was with who and what was actually going to happen. They had me completely off guard and so confused I was almost afraid to say anything.

Two hours ago, I was sure I knew who was who. Now I find that maybe I didn't know my left from my right. I had to slow things down a bit and get my bearings. "All right, hold everything here. Let me get a few things straight in my mind. First off, when I was working at the Mid Atlantic Group, they really were under the direct influence of the Cyclers?"

Tammy put her hand on the back of mine. "That's right."

"Then I was right when I discovered that paper. Beatrice Melenkowskie was a real person who suffered a real attack by the Cyclers and lost her life?"

Tammy again responded. "That is right."

I was making head way, but knew I only had minutes left. "Then this whole series of events I have been involved in over the past several weeks or months have been carefully planned in order to get me here, in this place, at this time?"

Again, Tammy was smiling and patting my hand. "That too is right."

Now I was getting a clearer picture. "So, you wanted me here specifically and for a specific purpose or reasons?"

Tammy leaned toward me and then looked at Mark. "Again, that is true.

"Larry, this is not the only facility of this kind here on Earth. However, it is the biggest and most important of the compounds they have been setting up in our dimension. You need to keep calm and remain as you are for the time being. We have to leave. They have the checkers coming to determine why you've been in this room all this time by yourself and have not come back out."

Tammy and Mark moved over in to the corner by the other side of the table and simply vanished. I saw nothing open or close. They were just gone. Just then the door opened and two men walked in.

First Man through the door looked the

room over and then spotted me. "Mister Manchester, are you here?"

I waved my hand at them. "Yes, over here in the corner."

He walked toward me and when he was close enough to actually see me. "Why are you here sitting in the dark?"

I sighed and stood up. "I'm thinking. I wanted to find a quiet place and just sit and think. I'm sorry, have I done something wrong?"

He was still looking around and checking the place out, "No, not in the least bit. It's just that it was noted you came in here and never came back out."

I played the dumb card. "Oh, I'm truly sorry. I have seen so much these past few weeks I needed to stop and get my head back on straight. I'll leave if you want me to."

The other man, who was still standing by the door, spoke up. "No, that's not a problem. We just wanted to make sure you were all right."

I spread both my hands and sat back down. "I'm just fine and thank you so much for your concern."

They both nodded and left the room. I sat there for maybe another five minutes and then got up and walked out, turning the lights off as I left. That old ticking in the back of my head was coming back. I was uneasy and was sure something was not as it should be. I was not sure who was who and that had me all screwed up something terrible?

I don't know, maybe I should stop thinking, but there is little I can do about it. My mind has to work on something and the Cyclers were always there, taking up my time. My mind would churn endlessly on how and when we should do this or that in dealing with them.

As I tried to determine who was against me and who was with me, I found myself being pulled in two, three and four directions. Was Reggie under the control of the Cyclers and Mark and Tammy were mistaken. For that matter, were they the Cyclers pawns? Everywhere I turned I was being given a different new perspective from someone.

But tonight, I was looking at the size and magnitude of the task that lay before us. That task of ending their seven thousand years of rule over this world and how we would do that. I don't mind telling you once I realized what I was thinking about I felt a sense of helplessness pass over me.

Everything created a feeling of doubt. And if I started to doubt myself then I was going to find myself hopelessly lost and probably dead. It was then I decided to keep my options open and to prepare myself for the unexpected.

Seven thousand years of dominance by these beings. It was so ingrained in this world I suddenly realized it was a near impossible, if not a totally impossible task. Who was under their control and who was free of it? How do you tell?

I continued thinking about how I could tell whether Reggie is controlled and Tammy and Mark are not? If I can't discern the difference then this situation is in fact impossible.

Mind you, I still wanted to do it, but I was having one of my reality phases and reality told me something ingrained like this could not be eradicated. If it was to be overcome it would have to be of their choice to leave, to drop all these years of dominance and leave us to our own.

No, it simply wouldn't do to fight them and drive them out. We had to hit them with something that made them more afraid of us than we are of them. Something so overwhelming all they could do was retreat, to re-evaluate their situation and get out of this arena of action. The problem was trying to determine just what that was.

Strange how things seem to happen and when they do, they actually fit in. There I am sitting in my room and thinking when the answer comes to me. I mean it just popped into my mind. It's that simple. I knew from the moment it came to me I had them and they would never be able to stop it. The key lay in my papers and I had to get to them and find the document I needed.

I left my room and went looking for Reggie. It took me about forty minutes to find him. He was working with a group of people on a new monitoring system designed to follow each individual on a one-on-one basis.

It was the ultimate monitoring system and when implemented no one would be able to have a single second of privacy. They would have every step you took nailed down.

As I walked up to them and thought about what they were doing, I decided I didn't like the implications of this new system and how it would impact everyone and me in particular. "Reggie, can I talk to you?"

He looked up and grabbed a rag and

walked over to me. "Sure Larry."

I looked over his shoulder at the others working on the system as he walked away from them and up to me.

He looked tired and a little rough around the edges. "Yeah, Larry, what can I do for you?"

I pointed at the cameras and people working on them. "Reggie, what the hell is that all about?"

He looked back over his shoulder and then back at me with a look of confusion on his face. "It's a new monitoring system we're trying to develop. We're having one hell of a time developing it. If I were to guess how long before we have it, I would say maybe three weeks to a month. We have to get it done and initiated in that time span."

I pressed the issue. "But, why is it necessary here and at this time?"

He stood there looking at me. I had the crawling feeling start up my back. "Larry, we think we may have been infiltrated. If that is true, we need to know what everyone is doing, it's vital."

With that I let it drop and then shifted over to my real reason for being there. "Reggie, I need to get to my papers."

He stopped wiping his hands off, "What for?"

I looked back at the cameras again and then the thought hit me, they had to have it done in three weeks to a month. That's all the time I had. "I think I have the answer, but I need to check my research first. I'll need around six hours with it. Can you work that out for me? I don't need to keep any of the papers, I just need to take a few notes I think apply to this situation."

Reggie looked down for a second and I could see he was not having any problem with my request. "Sure, you can take all the time you need. We need to complete the new monitoring system and the implementation of it, so I can't leave here at this time. Hanna."

A young woman stood up and walked over to where we were at. "Yes Reggie."

He reached out and took her by the arm. "Would you take Larry to his papers and personal items and let him in to work on some research he needs to do?"

She smiled at me and turned and started off down the hallway, "Sure, this way Larry."

As I followed Hanna I asked. "How long she had been here?"

She said she had just come into the

facility in the last three months.

She was really new here and may be just what I am looking for, but I needed to remain careful and not push things too hard. "How do they determine who should be here?"

She stopped and turned to me. "For me it was my tendency to reject the advice and directives of my parents and our friends."

That was strange, I thought. She was here because of her action or the way she acted with others. "How are you doing now?"

She smiled. "Just fine I hope I will be able to leave in a month or so."

That was again odd, why would they bring her here and then after just a few months let her out knowing full well when she left, she took all her knowledge of this place with her. Why would she want to leave? Does she really know what this place is or is there something else here?

This one appeared to be an innocent kid with little knowledge as to what was going on here, or she was one hell of a good actor. I made a note to talk to Reggie about her.

Hanna stood there a minute. "Strange, I really don't remember what it was that made everyone so angry with me. I can remember them being angry, but the reason for me slips my mind. I guess that's a good thing, but I'm not sure. All I know is something terrible happened and then I found myself here.

"They have been so good to me; I just love them. Here's the room your papers are in, please do not remove any of them. You can take notes, but all the documentation must remain in the room. Do you understand?"

Now I knew she was just doing as Reggie told her, but these were my papers and I felt I could take them, any or all, if I wanted to. Yet, I knew she was doing what she was being told and I let it drop. "Yes, I do and thank you Hanna."

As she started to turn to walk away, she hesitated a second, and appeared to almost say something then changed her mind and left me at the door.

I walked over to the table and started looking though the papers. It had to be here. They took everything so it had to be here. After a few minutes I found it. There it was the Milankovitch Cycles paper. The answer was there and had been there since 1941.

I sat down and started reading. As I stated before, Milankovitch's papers were a cosmological paper. It dealt with the cycles of our planet and solar system, and that was the key to all these issues. It was the ways and means of eliminating the Cyclers and ensuring they not return at anytime in the future.

Believe it or not, the key was the alignment of the planets. That's right, straight out of the astrologist notebook. It all had to do with gravitational influences here on earth, the gravity of the sun, the moon, and the other planets over the environment of earth. It was this, gravitational pressure that would ensure the impact on the population of planet Earth. If my calculations were right, that pressure would create difficulties for the Cyclers and in turn would open them up and make them vulnerable to our attack.

If we work everything right, they would abandon this dimension so fast the backlash would cause untold individual damage and injury, mostly mental.

But that is the price we will pay for our freedom. It will be impossible to separate us from the Cyclers without causing a lot of injury, both to them and to us.

The really interesting thing about this is it can be implemented by one person and not a group. The only coordination needed is the dealing with the cosmological cycles I will be applying. What I knew now was Cyclers lived by the manipulating of the biological cycles of their victims. The truth of the matter was they lived and died by that activity. If they fail to control, they are controlled and that is their Achilles Heel. That's where I've got them.

It took me almost five hours to complete my research. I wrote some notes down because that's what they were expecting. What I really needed to know I put into my mind and it would be there until that moment when I would apply what I knew they could not avoid.

I would still need the help of the underground here but I would only need two or three and not all. That would reduce the level of risk I was facing.

I also knew I would have to have free access to every area of this facility, unhampered access. That was going to be a major problem, but I had a plan for that as well. As near as I could tell, the facility had around four hundred occupants. That is a lot of people to deal with, but the overall size of the facility was such those four hundred did not fill even a third of the space.

Next, I knew this was an enclosed, self-maintained facility. Its air was circulated and filtered, with only a fraction coming from outside at any given time. The water was totally self-contained and controlled from within. This place could take a direct nuclear hit and still function. For me that was good, really good.

As they say, it only takes one bad seed to make a whole batch of seeds go bad. Well, I'm that bad seed and boy was I going to make a mess of this place.

When I was done, we would know who the good uncontrolled people were and who the bad were. I would be separating the two sides and one of them would never recover. I had a good feeling about some of the people, they were, in fact, good people. But there were others who appeared to put on a good front I had serious doubts about. In a short time, I would know who was who.

Right now, I needed someone I could depend on. By that I mean someone I could give a task to and know it would be carried out. Someone who was actually free of their control, that put Reggie out, and Mark. I considered including Hanna, but dropped that. She had been too obedient to Reggie when taking me to my papers. No, the one person I needed was Tammy Lake, and she was going to be in it up to her neck.

Yes, I know. How did I know Tammy was free of Cyclers control? Well, I didn't and that was my reasoning to use her. I had one thing working for me. I knew where I was in this overall game. I knew I was not controlled and in fact they, the Cyclers, would just love to get their hands on me. That put me right in the middle of the two sides and that was my advantage.

At dinner, I entered the dining hall and looked around. Sure enough, I saw Tammy sitting at a table on the far side of the hall with two other young ladies. I got my tray and food and then slowly walked in her direction. As I walked, I stopped and greeted several people I had come to know over the past few days, but maintained my steady movement toward Tammy.

When I finally got to her table she looked up and seemed a bit surprised to see me.

That was good. It meant she had not expected to see me so soon after our last meeting. Besides, I needed her in that surprised state. "Hi Tammy, may I join you."

She looked at her friend and then nodded her head, "Please do." As I sat down the two other girls got up and walked away.

I wanted them to leave and was happy to see they were in fact leaving, but I also needed to play the innocent thing. "Oh, please don't go. I'm sorry if I interrupted your conversation."

Both assured me they had things they needed to do and pardoned themselves and left.

I looked at Tammy, "I'm really sorry if I interrupted something."

She sat there, almost smiling and with a look I had caught the cat with the canary in its mouth. "No, no you didn't, believe me. How are you doing Larry?"

"I'm doing just fine. I have been able to get some research done and find I am making great headway."

Her expression changed and became more serious. "What are you working on Larry?"

Right question, and so I continued. "Well Tammy, maybe you don't really want to know."

She looked around and leaned forward toward me. "Larry, this is not the place to talk about anything outside of normal operational activities, too many ears."

Man, she worked right into the scenario so well I almost thought it was a put on. "Hold on Tammy, it's not like that. This is just straight on research I have wanted to do for a long time. I have no problem with anyone hearing about it."

She sat back and looked at me. I knew I had thrown her a curve, but I needed to see her reaction. What was she going to do? We were at a critical point in time and depending on how she reacted to me in the next few minutes would determine whether I would be able to actually carry out my plan.

I started to eat my meal as she sat there watching me and running everything, I had just said through her mind. Finally, she picked up her spoon and started eating her soup.

She had eaten some of her soup and then looked up at me. "Larry, would you like to go on a date with me tonight?" That was the right answer.

That was it, that was what I needed and she played it perfectly. I simply love these intrigue games; I think I'm great at them and when I set a person up, they do so well at it. "Well, if you don't have anything going, I would love to take a long walk with you if that would be all right."

She nodded her head and continued to eat. "That would be a pleasant and relaxing thing to do. There are a number of places throughout this facility that are wonderful locations to visit."

That was what I wanted to see, the rest of this facility, or as much of it as I could in what time we would have. "So far all I've seen of this place has been business. I was wondering if there were any recreational activities provided."

She set her spoon down and looked right at me. "Larry, I did not realize you had not seen any of our fun places. Please forgive us for neglecting that need for you. Yes, there are a number of fun and shopping places in this facility. In fact, I think you'll be pleasantly surprised at what you will see."

Just then Reggie walked up. "What are you two up to?"

Tammy looked up at Reggie and leaned back in her seat. "Larry just asked me out on a date, how about that?"

Reggie looked puzzled, "A date?"

Just then I chimed in. "Yeah, I felt like I needed some time away from all the craziness going on around me and so I thought of Tammy and came over here and asked her out for the evening, do you think that will be all right?"

Reggie smiled at me and then Tammy. "Now, don't keep him out too late young lady. He still has things to do and things to get ready for, understand."

Tammy laughs. "Reggie, we'll make it a short date."

Now was the time to play along with the conversation. I didn't know which one of these two were with me or against me, but I needed to let them both know I was oblivious to any issues that may be between them, whether they knew it or not. "Hold on lady, I don't want it too short, understand."

She looked over at me and smiled. "Whatever you want Larry."

Reggie looked at both of us. "I guess you two must have a thing going between you."

We both looked at each other and nodded at which point Reggie turned and left.

We finished our meals without saying much after that. It was approaching seven and we felt we had lots of time to walk around the facility and get a real good look at everything. As we left the dining hall Tammy suggested we go left and start at the shopping area.

As we walked, I looked the monitoring system over and realized it was more extensive than I had first thought. I could see no areas that were not covered by at least one camera and most were covered by two or three. That meant trouble for us when we started to make the move. But first I needed to find and consider the mechanical systems and locations for the facility.

We moved through the shops and then on down to the entertainment area. They had almost anything you wanted in the place and every bit of it was closely watched. At this point I determined I needed to start asking some touchy questions. "Tammy, where have you worked your passages in?"

She thought for a minute and evidently decided to give me something. "Most of them are within the buildings themselves. None open onto the traffic ways in that everything has multiple cameras on them. There are numerous areas inside the buildings that do not have as complete a coverage."

That was interesting in that if they had stayed with their open area concepts and extended it into the buildings as well, they would have covered the inside areas the same way. "What is the extent of your ability to move through the facilities by those means?"

She was being careful, in that I was not a proven security risk to her yet, "Extensive Larry. We can move in just about any location without being monitored."

I then decided I needed to check the level of security they were using within their own group. "How sure are you that Mark is in fact on your side?"

She stood there looking at me. "I'm not totally sure Larry. There have been a number of indications that tells me he is really just playing us along."

I listened to her and then added. "So, Mark is a questionable person in the overall scheme of things?"

She nodded to me. "That, I would say is a yes."

We moved on down the walk way, my mind was charging ahead of me like a wild animal. "Then we will no longer work with Mark around."

She did not like what I said, but she nodded again. "All right, but that might alert him to our activity."

I was not happy with her response. It seemed she did not want to leave Mark out, but to placate me she agreed. I continued.

"Not if we simply leave him out and make it look like we're engaged in our relationship and not an attack on this facility."

Now I wanted to know what she knew and Mark was a great topic to check that on. "Is there anything specific you can point to in regards to your questions concerning Mark?"

She thought for a few seconds and turned to me. "The new injected monitor/tracker system is one example. He said he was trying to delay it, but it continues to progress."

That was a good example, and it was most interesting to me. "You said Mark's involved in that?"

She was thinking hard and fast and then continued. "Yes, he builds and assembles the electronics that are involved. Nothing has happened that would stop it and nothing really has delayed it. That system will be starting up in about a month, right on schedule."

I noted her concern and watched her eyes. They were still dead, not showing much of anything you would think would be jumping right out at you. "When it does, then what?"

She shrugged her shoulders. "Then we are no longer a threat to the Cyclers."

That was vital information, but it still did not confirm one way or the other as to who were actually the Cyclers or the associates. "All right, then that means we must implement my plan before then."

She turned and looked right at me. "Larry, how do you know you can trust me?"

I smiled and noted the deadness in those eyes and told her. "Tammy, I don't. However, I have a greater sense of trust in you than I do in Reggie or anyone else in this place."

With that she changed the subject. "How many people are you going to need to implement your plan?

I took a hold of her elbow and steered her down the walkway, "Just you and I Tammy, just you and I."

She stopped again and looked right at me. "No way, how can that be? This place is crawling with people that in minutes can be directed to remove you from the facility and eliminate you."

I wanted to see her reaction and agreed with her assumption as to what could happen. "That's true, but the fact it's just the two of us is in our favor. They expect a massive attack by a third of the facilities personnel. They're not going to get that. It will be just two and that is all we need."

By this time, I had her really confused, "Larry, how?"

I put her off at that time, preferring to let that part of the plan sit for a while, "Not yet Tammy, not yet. I will let you know minutes before it starts and by then you will understand completely just what is going on and happening.

"Right now, I need to know the locations of the control center, the water treatment facility and the air exchange system. Take me around, but do it as random as you can. Let's take a walk out and look at the dome and just talk about anything and everything. You know nothing special, a guy and a gal together spending some special time with one another."

She was still not happy with being left out of the planning and its details. "All right, if that's what you want."

With that she stopped and stepped up to me and put her arms around my neck and gave me a kiss I had not felt for I don't know how many years. You know, one of those kisses that strip the wind out of you. You almost stagger under it, but the feeling resulting from it could make you run a mile, full bore.

We figured we had another three hours before someone would start to ask questions as to when we plan on pulling the plug and returning to our rooms. They did not have a curfew, but they did discourage being out of your room after eleven, kind of an unofficial curfew.

We finally came to the control center. It was just inside from where their vehicles were parked outside the building in the dome. As you entered the building, instead of going straight you go to the left and there is a tee junction. To the right are double doors and that is the control center. To the left were administrative offices and Tammy took me that way to show where Reggie's office was.

We found a directory and stopped and looked at it for a few minutes as I orientated myself to this area. Then we returned to the tee and went back the way we came. No attempt was made to approach the control center. I knew where it was and that's all I needed at this time.

Our next target was the water treatment facility. That proved to be a little more difficult. We managed to get to the main tunnel that led back to the plant, but could go no further without being contacted by guards. The same was true for the air quality control system. But I knew where they were and I found the main piping and conduit that came from and went to those facilities.

Once we achieved that task, we returned to the entertainment area and found a bench outside in the square and sat down. We talked about our lives and how we came to be here in this place and found our stories were not that much different.

She had been an investigative reporter and had found herself following a trail of missing people and finding they all had common ties. As she moved further into her investigation, she felt she was being watched. It was during this time she had been contacted by a lady professor out of the University of Illinois about some kind of inter-dimensional invasion by something called Cyclers.

I looked at her and simply said, "Beatrice Melenkowskie."

Her mouth dropped open. She sat there and looked down and then back at me and into my eyes. "Where did you know her?"

I had hit something big in Tammy and she was reacting. This was more reaction to that remark than she had demonstrated all evening, except maybe the kiss. "I was with the Mid Atlantic Group and had received an assignment to review a paper she had submitted. It was a terrible paper, nothing like it should have been. I could not put it down and started to follow up on it when I was hauled out here."

She sat there and looked at me. I could tell I had hit on something by her reaction. "That's how it happened to me. I was trying to make an appointment with the dean at her college and when I left my meeting with him, they took me."

Now it was my turn to be surprised. "Now that's interesting. It was shortly after I met with Dean Singer, they took me."

She seemed to drift off for a moment. "Yeah, stay away from Dean Singer."

I was finally at the point of having seen and heard much more than I thought I could deal with by this time, "Tammy, let's call it a night."

Her reaction to that was more pleasant than everything else we had been through so far that evening, well, except for the kiss. "Now, but Larry, we were just starting to get into things."

Now I had to demonstrate my self control and bring this evening to an end. "I know, but we have been together for four hours and they seem too not like that. I feel we need to break it off now and then get together for breakfast and figure out our next move. Right now, we need to be careful. This whole thing is between you and I and no one else understand."

It made me feel good to see her wanting the evening not to end. "Are you sure Larry?"

I wanted so much to agree with her, but I had to stay on my plan and schedule. "Believe me Tammy, I would prefer the evening not end, but we must be disciplined and stay with the plan. What is going to happen only requires the two of us, and right now we cannot jeopardize that plan. Anything else that could interfere in the process would be a problem, all right?"

She shrugged. "That's fine with me."

I nodded, knowing full well I did not want the evening to end, but it had to. "Okay, let's call it a night. I'll walk you back to your apartment and then see you in the morning."

Then she smiled and reached out and took my hand. "We could spend the night together?"

Damn, she played the sex card and that is one move I find almost impossible to resist, but my goal was burned into my mind and I was going to stay with it. "Tammy, you're pushing me. No, you're tempting me and we can't do it right now."

She pushed the idea and moved in close. "Aw Larry, they won't care and I really do care."

Crap, this is getting out of hand and I could feel myself wanting to be with her. "Me to, but let's fight the wants and pursue the needs."

She looked at me and pouted. "If you say so, but when this thing is all over you had better be ready, understand?"

I smiled at her and then pulled her close up against me. "That I do, that I do. And, I look forward to it as well."

She leaned back and looked me in the eyes and giggled, "Really?"

I nodded my head and laughed. "Oh Tammy, if you only knew." I then pulled her to me and gave her a return kiss that matched the one she threw at me earlier.

I left her at her apartment and walked the short distance to mine. As I walked up to my door, I heard something inside the room. I paused and gave them time to clear out and then opened the door and stepped in. The room looked to be as I left it, but even the best of them cannot absolutely leave a room as it was, and these people did not.

The notes I had written down were out of order, and they had been returned to the table in the wrong position. I was curious as to where the secret passageways were and decided to look the room over. It took me most of the night, but I finally found it and the key to opening it up. Because I knew my room was monitored, I did not open the passage and left things as they were.

They had read the notes and that would lead them off in a direction away from me and my plans. There was little doubt they were concerned about me and that made me wonder why they simply did not eliminate me. There had to be a reason, but for the time being I had no idea. And with that I would carry out my plan and finish this thing once and for all.

Over the past few hours, I had made good headway on my plan. I had not put myself in a position where I could be compromised by either side. I knew I could have things backward or turned around.

Whatever the case I knew one side was Cycler controlled and the other was the resistance. In time I would know which was which, but for now I had a plan and I was going to carry it out.

Chapter Seven

PLANS COME TOGETHER

I had in my mind the way of achieving my goal. What I did not have right then were the means of that achievement. I knew I would be using either the water system or the air system as my primary attack weapon. I needed to put the whole of the facility down, either knocked out or killed. That was hard to think about, but the people within this facility must be neutralized.

I needed to be able to move around the facility and the one person who could help me in that way was Tammy. Had I picked the right person? Was she truly with me or was she solid with the Cyclers? I had to set up a contingency plan in the event she was my enemy and I dearly prayed she was not. Again, I needed to stay in the middle and not lean too far to one side or the other. Everyone was suspect and no one was exempt.

My first need was my weapons for attacking the facility. I would be using gas in the air or a solution in the water. The air was the best selection because everyone is dependent on air every minute of every hour. So, I decided to work on the air system.

With that I needed to come up with a gas that could be made from the chemicals that would be commonly used in a facility such as this. My problem was I must determine whether it was disabling or fatal.

The need regarding the disabling or fatal issue was another test I was building into my planning system. Anyone who was still affiliated with those who are fighting the Cyclers would lean toward the disabling gas and not a fatal gas.

On the other hand, anyone who would be with the Cyclers would have no opposition to my using a fatal gas. That was the key in my making sure Tammy was actually on my side and not an enemy. I truly prayed she was with me and not just using me.

Next, it had to be odorless whether

disabling or fatal. They could not be forewarned of a problem. It had to hit them straight on and put them down. Then I needed some form of protection for myself and Tammy. That called for a gas mask of some type. Surely, they had gas masks in this place somewhere. I would depend on Tammy to find them and bring them to me.

Now I needed to consider the monitoring of my room. I was sure they had both video and sound monitoring of me while I was in my room. That meant my room had to become a point of subterfuge, a place where I could work on my ideas, and they believed were my real activities, and not what I was actually up to. My notes had been the first move in creating that subterfuge.

I would have to work with Tammy to find a place where I could work in relative security in building my gas bombs and planning their placement. I was sure I would never be able to get to the actual air exchange air return location, so I figured I would have to use the overall system to infuse the gas into the facility, the whole of the base.

Now the big questions, what kind of gas, how do I produce it, and where do I set it off? Those three questions were the greatest issue I would have to face. If I found and selected the right one, I could set it off anywhere in the air return system and then wait for it to hit and take effect.

That is if I could do it with just one bomb. If not then I would need as many duct locations as I had bombs. My task would become much harder. I knew this; I would need one of the heavy metal toxins, such as Arsenic, Antimony or Bismuth. Next, I would need a strong acid such as sulfuric or hydrochloric acid. The sulfuric being the more preferred.

I would need to calculate the amount of the heavy metal and acid I would need to fill the whole of the facilities air system full of the toxic gas. If successful the end result would likely be a one hundred percent fatality rate for over four hundred people.

Wait, that's plain crazy. I can't do that, but I can make Tammy think I am doing that. I needed to keep her off guard in the event she was not what I thought she was. If she went along with me, then I would be fairly certain she was not on my side.

My other alternative would be Carbon Monoxide or Carbon Dioxide both of which act slowly and are just as deadly, but take longer to achieve that point. That would give us time to act on the Cyclers and then infuse clean air into the facility and save the lives of everyone in the place.

One methodology was fast and almost sure of neutralizing the place. The other methodology was slow and gave us a chance of reviving everyone before high levels of toxic effect takes place. It was a hard decision, but it had to be one or the other.

Yes, I could opt for a non-lethal gas, but many of those gases are not effective enough to take out the whole of an enclosed location and still some would die no matter what. On top of that Tammy would not have to worry about blowing her cover, if she was on the wrong side.

No, I really had no choice. My resources were limited and I would have to go for the knockout punch right off the bat. I had to use the heavy metals for my gas bomb. If Tammy proves to be what she says she is, then I will have to take this base out in total. I was playing a terribly close game and if I failed to read her right, I could literally destroy the only formidable force on earth to deal with the Cyclers. Everything was on the line.

The next morning, I met Tammy at the dining hall. As I sat down, she reached over and touched my hand.

She looked like she had slept well and was eager to get going. "You don't look like you slept at all."

She was observant and appeared to really be concerned for me. "You're right I didn't, after your desire to share the night with me, I found it hard to sleep after I decided not to and left. Now, can you tell me if there is a supply of acid here on the base?"

She didn't want to get right down to business, and reached over to touch me. "You should have come back instead of suffering all night like that. Anyway, she continued, yes there is. We use it in a lot of our projects for etching and other metal preparations."

That was perfect. It appeared they had a large supply of the chemical. "Good, is it sulfuric, and how much can you get for me."

She was looking at me with a confused look in her eyes. "Gallons, there is no restrictions in its use for those projects."

I continued to pursue the issue. "Do you have access to any chemicals, like any heavy metals and such?"

She was starting to really look

concerned. "No, that's a little out of our area of use. But there are supplies of arsenic available through the supply store."

Bingo, I had hit the jackpot. "Perfect, how do I get a supply of that stuff?"

She sat there and looked down at the breakfast and then back at me. "That my dear Larry, I'm not sure of."

I let that pass on by and pushed the issue. "Well, you need to find out and then let me know how much you can get at any one time."

She settled back. "All right, then we will work on that."

I was batting a thousand and decided to go for the next need. "Do you have access to gas masks?"

She was nodding her head as if she was finally tying everything together. "Yes, a few, but not a lot. Larry what are you up to?"

That was the limit, I now had to start explaining myself and see what came from that. So far, she has gone along with me; the next few minutes will tell me everything. "Tammy in order to take out the Cyclers, we must neutralize this facility. That means we must knock it down completely. Take everyone out even if we have to kill them."

She looked at me like I was crazy. "Larry, we can't do that."

I listened to her. "Yes, we can hon. in fact we have to."

She came back with an alternative. "What if we set the bombs up to try and make everyone sick as hell?"

I shook my head and looked into her eyes. "Tammy, we need thirty minutes to carry out the attack on the Cyclers. That means the gas bombs have to immobilize everyone without a gas mask for that time period or longer. Preferably forty-five to sixty minutes."

So far, I liked her response. "On top of that, some of these people are lethal. They will hunt us down and kill us as fast as they can. We must hit them with everything we can muster and that must be with the most toxic weapon we can put together.

"Now, if you're with me you understand what I am saying and you will assist me. If you are still Cyclers controlled then you will turn me over to Reggie right now."

That set the trap and now I would wait and see what she would do.

I had put everything on the line. She

was either going to help me or kill me, one or the other. She had no other choice. She sat there looking at me.

I could see the confusion in her eyes. "Larry, you're not fair. You know I can't go on without you. Yes, I know we must hit them and hit them hard and I know there is no other way we can do it. The fact is there are few of us in this place. Reggie has played along with us just to amuse himself, but he is fully Cyclers controlled and has no desire to see it any other way.

"Mark is still under their control and he does anything and everything they tell him to do, even becoming one of us so they can keep track of us. I've known for almost as long as I've been here. I have my own set of private doors and ways of getting around this place. So, it's time we actually do something about them."

I found myself with my mouth wide open. "Tammy, that's cold as heck. You really know how to make a guy feel inadequate. Who's running this outfit anyway?"

She smiled and leaned toward me. "Larry, we have a lot to do, so don't get too relaxed. I have a feeling all hell is about to break loose, so let's get with it."

She had walked through the door and now the show was on.

Over the next three days we were together almost continuously. We played the lovers card to the hilt. Not that we weren't, it's just we were in love and we were going to kill this place and the Cyclers hold on this world.

Finally, we were ready to set a date. As we walked and talked, we came up with the perfect day and that was a Tuesday. That worked out to be the slowest, most inactive day of the week consistently. The next jobs were the bombs themselves.

I figured we would need enough toxic gas to fill over forty-five rooms of varied sizes. Getting the gas to the rooms was the trick and we had that worked out. Every room in the facility had its own cooling and heating inlet and outlet. The inlets were located either in the ceiling or upper walls and the outlets were at floor level.

Because of the security at the air control center, we felt the best approach was to introduce the gas via the outlet air return system. That would determine the actual and necessary size of each bomb. Our plan was to make enough bombs for placement into half the outlet spots in the facility.

At the same time Tammy was starting to collect the arsenic we would use. We figured one ounce of arsenic per bomb and it would take two cups of sulfuric acid to convert the arsenic into a gas. The air system would then suck it in and run it through the output system and fill the base with a lethal dosage of gas.

She could collect around three ounces of arsenic per day and in two weeks we would have enough for fourteen bombs. I figured that would be ample to do the job. Once we started to assemble them there was no turning back. It would take several hours to do that and we needed to time our actions carefully.

We decided the best way to get that done and initiate the assault was to do it when we decided to spend our first night together. In that case we would use the cycles they depended on to control us as our excuse to sleep together. Sex can be a great cover-up for a lot of other activity.

Gas masks would become a major issue for us. They had some masks on the base, but those were restricted to the mechanical areas of the base and we did not have access to them. So, we designed and built them ourselves. We had two needs; one was to avoid breathing the gas in and the other was to protect our eyes.

Goggles were readily available throughout the base. They were used everywhere for protection in just about any activity. The breathing issue was the more difficult problem. That we took care of with two tampons and a couple of plastic bags and tape, crude, but workable. All we had to do was get to the control center and we knew they had good gas masks there.

Finally, we had it all ready except for the one thing that would be the weapon of choice for the Cyclers and that was the secret from Milankovitch's paper, the means of driving them back to their dimension and not ever coming back. I felt I could have that part ready in about three days. With the plan all set up and detailed all we would have to do is to wait for the Tuesday of choice to come.

The astrologers of the world would have been proud of me. I had the day and time for the alignment worked out and it fit in perfect with what we were planning. If all worked out, it would counter the environment of the other dimension and give us a chance at making this thing happen.

As we completed the collection of our

supplies and the final location of the air ducts we would be using, we had it all together and ready to go. I sat there looking at Tammy knowing what was to come would be hard on both of us, but the need clearly outreached our personal feeling.

It was simply a necessity and just the idea of killing all these people, hurt. It made no difference whether they were Cycler controlled or not it was the idea we were going to kill everyone.

My other problem was that Tammy was deeply involved in making that thing happen and that was bad news to me. I still couldn't say she was controlled, but I had a deep foreboding she was and that would mean all we had done so far was actually targeted on the Cyclers enemy and not the Cyclers.

Chapter Eight

THE CYCLERS WEAPON

We knew that mirrors or any reflective surface could be used by the Cyclers to observe our dimension. We also knew they could send gargoyles through those mirrors and they in turn could kidnap and kill targeted people in this dimension.

I was able to block their access into this dimension by placing another mirror facing the first mirror and thereby creating a reversal of anything they tried. I had a good idea what it did to the gargoyles or to their attempt to observe us, and I knew it stopped them cold.

I then continued my research and determined their hold over us was through our biological cycles all living creatures have. Just how they did that I did not know, but they did and it was effective. However, it was clear some people were not controlled by them.

For some reason we, me included, had some kind of resistance to their attempts to control us individually. So, they tried to control us through the governments of the worlds that they did control.

If we became too great a threat, they would then send in the gargoyles to either kill or kidnap us. That brought up a question about this base or facility, if they ran it why no mirrors?

I assumed they used the video camera system and they may well do that, but there seemed to be something wrong there. The lack of mirrors was the key and there were none. If it was in fact a Cyclers base, it would have Cyclers access capabilities and the lack of mirrors eliminated that.

I settled into my room that night and started to think things over again. This was getting just too darn complex and I needed to figure out where the heck I was at, if I could. I had sat down in the corner of the room away from the monitoring camera in the book case. It was later while sitting there I felt something was wrong, something I had overlooked.

I had been sitting there maybe an hour

when I felt a presence in the room. I knew there was access to my room from a secret panel and I had expected visitors in time. The problem was I was not sure who that would be and right now that made little difference. There was something there. I heard nothing and saw nothing I just knew there was a presence.

I froze in place and waited. I did not dare move. I felt if something was there it needed me to give myself away in order for it to zero in on me. So, I sat there and brought my breathing down to as low and slow a level as I could. I thought to myself I had been fortunate in not going to bed because whoever or whatever was in the room would be looking to the bed to find me.

It was moving around across the room near my desk. I could just barely make something out. When the hell did it come through the panel, I had heard nothing? The room was black as it could get. With no windows there is no light source except for the light fixtures when they're turned on. The room was black except for the digital clock on the desk and a small light in the kitchen, yet I could make out a black form near my desk. Yeah, it was there, slowly moving around the desk and searching out the area looking for me.

I had heard in a black environment a solid object can be seen simply because it is blacker than the black around it. Black space is lighter than a solid black object. Once your eyes become accustomed to the black you can then make out differences in the shades of black on black.

I sat there and watched it for some time. Each move was deliberate and calculated. After a few minutes I started to notice things about that figure that were familiar to me. Yeah, I knew this creature and I was now finding out a few things I wished I was not learning. I had been betrayed and my life was on the line. I had set myself in the middle and now I was getting answers to my questions. Just that the answers were not what I wanted them to be.

It had to know I was there, but it was concentrating on my desk and appeared not to be looking for me. Yet, I was right there. No something was wrong with this whole thing. She was right there looking over my desk and area around it. Not really looking for me, but I felt sure if I presented myself, I would be fighting for my life in short order.

Finally, she moved over by my bed and when she realized I was not in it she froze. Now she was looking for me. Now she knew I was a threat to her. Now the real confrontation was going to take place. You could feel the emotions and the danger spread across the room.

Why had she waited this long to come after me? Better yet, what was it I had done to cause her to make a move on me at this time and not later? I needed to bring this thing to head. This had been what I wanted to know, who was who and which side was I actually on. I was about to find out. "Tammy, what are you doing here?"

She spun around and just as she was facing me, I turned the lights on. She stood there shaking her head.

Her hands were clutched into fists and she was trembling. She knew she had been caught and we were at a point when everything was going to come out. "You should have been sleeping Larry. Now I'll have to do something I was hoping I would never have to do."

I sat there watching her and as long as I could keep her attention on me the better my chances of surviving this confrontation were.

"What is that, Tammy? Killing me?"

She was now concentrating on me so hard her face was flaming red and I knew something was driving her that was beyond her control or my understanding. "Larry, I have no choice. It has taken us years to infiltrate this base and set it up for elimination and you were going to be our tool to accomplish that. But you've found me out and that means I have to eliminate you now.

"I have no choice; it simply has to be. I wish it could be some other way, but the stakes are too high for you to be permitted to simply walk away. Besides, you know too much and you're dangerous to the Cyclers."

Deep down inside I had known this was the way this was going to end up. Too many things pointed to her, the lack of mirrors in the facility, the extra hidden passageways, and the way she aligned herself with me and seemed willing to hang Mark out to dry. Now it was coming together and for this she was going to kill me, well try too anyway. "Tammy, may I ask one thing?"

You could see her preparing herself to take me on. For a moment she relaxed. "What's that?"

I had her total and complete attention

now and continued. "Why did you come here? You had to know it was a high-risk action? So, why now?"

She shook her head and looked down at the floor and then back at me. "We thought you may have seen the error I made last night when we were walking around."

What error was she talking about? Was that what was bothering me, something I knew was wrong, but could not put a finger on. "I saw no error, Tammy. Up until now, I was preparing to complete the attack we had planned."

She seemed surprised and a little bewildered, "Really?"

I started to relax now, the end was coming nearer and I could do nothing about it. "That's right. I was sitting here going over everything when you came in. You came here to cover your ass and if need be, to kill me. This is not a Cyclers base is it, Tammy? It is just as Reggie said it was and you have been sent to try to gain access to this place and if possible, destroy it. You almost did that, with my help. That probably hurts more than anything else that has happened to me over the past several months.

"You're the perfect weapon. You come

here under their complete control and infiltrate the base, find a gullible man and through him wipe the base out or at least set it up for a Cyclers invasion. The problem with that dear Tammy is you failed. I hate to say this but you're not going to leave this room alive and that is going to hurt me to the core.

"One other thing Tammy, I knew when I came here there was probably a degree of infiltration by the Cyclers. On my first day here Reggie and I talked about the probability of there being Cycler agents on the base and the need to find them and remove them. Tammy, that was my first task here at the base, to find out who the Cycler agents were and take them out."

You could see the sudden realization cross her face. She knew now she had walked into a trap and she was going to be fighting for her life and not to take mine. "Larry!"

I stopped her from saying anything else. It was time and it was something that had to be done. There was no way around it and for that I knew I would probably never live this down. "No Tammy, it's over. Reggie!"

She spun around again and Reggie hit her right across the throat with such a blow that knocked her clear onto the bed. I sat there watching her as she turned her head toward me. She lay there looking at me and I saw her lips move, "Larry, I'm sorry." The blood started to run out of her mouth and in less than a minute her eyes went glassy and closed.

All I could do was sit there and look at her. We had only known each other for a few days and I had come to love her. For that the Cyclers would pay dearly. They would pay like none other on this world has paid by their presence here. The hate welled up in me and I knew this was now a fight to the finish and I was willing to die to get there. They would pay, I promised myself they would pay.

Reggie opened the door and two men came in and picked her up and carried her out of the room. He walked over and sat down beside me.

This was a man of great compassion and even greater drive to overcome the rule of the Cyclers. He put his hand on my shoulder. "Larry, I am truly sorry for this. If there is any way I can help you just let me know."

The tears were freely running down my face and I could feel myself wanting to melt into a heap on the floor. I looked at Reggie. "Thanks Reg, "Oh, what about Mark?"

Reggie looked over at the door as one of the men returned. "He'll be dealt with and taken into custody." The man nodded and then turned and left with the other man standing in the hall.

Finally, I started to come around. Now I was mad as hell and the level of hate was building in me was almost more than I could take. "Right now, there is nothing I want more than to get at those Cyclers and I think it's time we started moving on that."

Reggie stood up and walked half way to the door and then turned, "You sure?" The look on his face was the same as I felt right then. We were attuned to each other and we both knew it.

I finally got up and walked over to my desk and picked up the notes. "Yes, I'm ready. Absolutely, I want nothing but to put them down and out of our lives, the sooner the better. Besides I have already identified the planet alignment and we need to attack at that time."

I could see Reggie's demeanor change. Those were the right words at the right time and he knew it. "All right Larry, if that's what you want then we had better get started. But first we need to retrieve that tracking seed from your hand."

I had forgotten all about that and so we went to the lab and had Teddy remove the seed.

As Teddy cut the seed out of my hand, I realized this seed was the first real tangible evidence I had ever seen that was a product of the Cyclers. That would become extremely important in time. "Don't destroy that, Teddy. We need to take it apart and see what kind of technology they have over on the other side."

Teddy smiled at me and put the seed into a small vile and placed that in his shirt pocket. "That I can assure you we will do Larry. Now is there anything else?"

I suddenly felt worn out, so tired I didn't think I could walk back to my room. "Not at this time."

What I had not known during this time with Tammy was Reggie had been working on my original plan all this time and he advised. "The two mirrors have been moved into the inner chamber that you wanted. The engineers have built the frame work for them and they will be mounted before noon tomorrow."

I took a second look at him. "You let me go through all of this and never even tried to tell me what you were up to?" I felt myself smiling. Damn, this was a good man and he had me pegged from the beginning. "Great, then we can start planning the actual capture process. Is everything else ready?"

By now Reggie had a smile covering his whole face. "Yes, we have a full perimeter warning system set up and active. The main tunnel entrance has been fortified and we feel we can hold off anything they throw at us. Your idea to try and smoke these agents out was great, but we didn't want to do anything that might show our hand. So, I went ahead and got things moving."

Then he got a little more serious. "Do you think they know where this base is?"

That brought me back to the current situation. "I'm not sure Reg, in all probability they do, otherwise they would not have sent Mark and Tammy in here. They would need someone on the inside to help in any attack they might launch against this place."

"But, what if they don't Larry?"

"We can't take any chances; we have to function with the belief they know we are here."

Reggie was watching me closely. "What are you thinking Larry?"

My mind was running five different directions all at the same time by now. "I guess I'm thinking about Tammy. I only wish it had not gone that way. She played a good game, but she was on the short end when she came in here."

He was nodding his head in understanding. "Larry, can I ask you a question?"

It was not a time to stop the dialog. "Sure, what is it?"

He walked over by the desk beside me. "When did you finally determine we were not a Cyclers base?"

Whether he believed me or not, "Oh, I knew that from the beginning."

That caught him by surprise and he turned and leaned over the desk, "How?"

I turned and sat on the desk dangling my feet off the floor. "Well, in a way it's simple, but then again easy to miss.

"It was the absence of the mirrors. They may be able to work with video monitoring, but they have to have direct access to their victims in the event they need to collect them or kill them for whatever reason. They have to have the mirrors to gain entry into this dimension. They have no other way. Video cameras do not give them that access.

"No, anywhere they have a power base they will have mirrors all over the place. It can be no other way. When Tammy started leading me down the path, she was agreeing with me this was a Cyclers base and then I knew she was one of them. Oh, by the way, may I suggest you carry out an in-depth autopsy on her before eliminating her."

By this time, he wanted to hear more. "That we will do, what else was there?"

I knew he would never let it rest until I laid everything out for him. "Let me know what you find. I would bet she is not of this dimension and it will help to see what they are made of. That would help greatly in our final push against them. She was one hell of a weapon and she almost got what she wanted.

"Now to continue, she was too agreeable with everything I said and that struck me as being odd. She knew nothing about me and so much as said so, and then she would turn around and act as if I was one of them. It was just out of place and not lining up right

"Oh, and our little talk before the initial meeting helped me in targeting her and Mark. You knew you were compromised and with me coming on the scene you finally had someone you knew was targeted by the Cyclers who you could use.

"I still wasn't sure as to your actual allegiance but after that talk I could concentrate on Tammy and Mark. It made all the difference in the world."

They say you never ever get used to seeing death. Well, they're wrong. Death is a tool and it can be used most effectively and efficiently when applied right. The more I have seen of these beings the more death has become an important tool in my arsenal. My feeling toward Tammy was true, but it appears she was not even of this dimension, whatever she was.

For that they would pay dearly. In the beginning I simply wanted them to go away. Now I want them to pay and pay dearly. It was no longer the overthrowing of an unwanted power. It was the annihilation of a heartless enemy. I wanted as many of them dead as possible. I was going to hit them with a means of killing more of them than they have ever experienced before.

I started the next leg of my assault on those beings, something I had been working on in the back of my mind for some time now,

"Reggie?"

"Yes, Larry."

I moved around to the desk chair and sat down. "How extensive are your scientific capabilities in this facility."

He knew something was about to come out of me that would mean his current plans were being redesigned. "Larry, we have probably some of the most advanced capabilities of anywhere else in the world. What are you looking for?"

That was what I wanted to hear because what I was about to come up with would be so far out, they would be straining just to keep up with what I wanted. "First of all, I need to know a few things. First, how do you feel toward the Cyclers?"

It sounded like a stupid question, but I needed to know just how far Reggie would be willing to go in our fight against them. "Larry, there is not enough hate left in the world to even began to match the level of hate I have for them. I have not told many people this, but those things killed my wife and children in an attempt to control me.

"I resisted and they took my family and without mercy they gave them over to the gargoyles and then made me stand there and watch what they did to them. I hear their screams every night in my sleep. When I hit Tammy, I did so with all the hate and drive I could put into it. Sorry about that, but I released a lot of pent-up anger in that one blow."

I now knew this man was going to be more than just a partner in this battle, he was going to be a primary force driving this fight. "You have no reason to be sorry about that Reg. She was on her side, we're on our side and we and they will give no quarters. Besides, what I have seen so far has caused me to develop a deep hate for them as well. Any means I can come up with to attack them I will use and use it with all the devastating force I can put into it."

It's really something how hate can drive a person. "Second, what did you do before coming here?"

He looked at me and it was like the lights had gone on and he got this little smile that settled in his lips. "I was the head of a weapons design and production facility in the Midwest. We worked on mass destruction weapons and chemical weapons at that facility."

Oh boy, this was going to be good.

"Third, do you have those capabilities here in this base?"

He now looked like a man who prided himself in his planning and readiness. "Larry, if I'm reading you right, I think you're going to do more than just separate us from them, you plan on leaving a real mess over on their side of the universe."

I felt the same kind of smile slide across my lips. "That sir is exactly what I plan on doing."

That's all it took, he moved into high gear. "All right, how do we do that? What is it you want?"

I think we were at a point in Reggie's life where he had had enough and knew it was time something was done, for that matter anything. I had to smile at his reaction and clear and present determination. "That sir will depend on whether we can capture one of theirs when it comes through the mirror. Once we get it, I want a complete biological study done on it and on Tammy's body as well. I want to know their weaknesses and I want to know if they are susceptible to contagions."

Reggie's eyebrows went up as he finally caught on to what I was up to. "You're planning on a germ attack."

I started nodding and looking through my notes. I had deliberately led everyone to the Milankovitch papers knowing full well that anything that had to do with the alignment of the planets was secondary to the primary attack. "Yes, I'm planning on an invasion of the worst kind. I want to hit them with not just one, but several bugs at once. They may be immune to some of our bugs and they may be able to eradicate some, but with any luck they will not be able to resist all of them."

He sat back and I could see his mind churning away. "So, the question is, can we take the body of Tammy and the second body of the captured creature and load them up with enough bugs and explosives that it will send the bugs all over the place."

"Reg that is another reason we need to get a look inside their dimension. Can they stop the spread of our bugs? If not, we have them. If they can then we will need to wipe out the base that is connected to us and prepare for future invasions from them."

He was already working up the schedule and necessary needs for an attack of this magnitude. "Then we'll need two of them from the other side."

Yeah, that's what I want, we needed an in-depth study of these beings and we needed it fast. "No, we have one in Tammy. Just one more will do. We will send Tammy back with a small cocktail of bugs and a bomb that is buried deep in her. But the captured one will go back with the video and sound capabilities we have been working on.

"Once, there we can get a good look at their situation and then if it looks good feed Tammy to them. As she goes in, I want to feed a tube in behind her and block the portal open and then start feeding bugs in mass. I want the feeding to be like a fire hose, except it needs to be even greater.

"That is where the Cycle weapon I found in Milankovitch's paper comes into play. We are approaching that cycle at this time and once were into it we can feed a huge amount of stuff through the portal into their dimension in short order."

He was a little confused by what I was saying. "How can that be?"

So, I decided he needed a little lesson on Milankovitch and his study of cycles. "There are three general force changes in the cycles of our solar system. The first is Eccentricity, which are the elliptical changes in the earth's orbit around the sun. Next is Obliquity, which is the tilt of the earth's axis toward and away from the sun. Third is Precession, the wobble of the earth's axis toward and away from the sun.

"These three issues bring about force changes on the Earth and that in turn creates forces that will impact the portals when they are opened. The two terms that Milankovitch cycles are increasingly involved with are Perihelion which is when the earth's northern hemisphere land mass is facing the sun and is the closest to the sun causing warming.

"Aphelion which is the opposite when the earth's northern hemisphere land mass is further from the sun and causing cooling. Both of these cycles directly relate to the climatic conditions here on earth and that involved the highs and lows of atmospheric high and low pressures.

"We are approaching the end of our solar system's orbit around the center of our galaxy. As they are in all galaxies, we have a super black hole at the center of ours. Though we will pass many light years from that black hole, it still creates huge levels of energy that will impact the Cyclers when that portal is held open. It will be almost like matter and anti-matter touching each other.

"Add the planetary alignment and the natural forces hitting that portal will create a situation where there is a lower pressure on their side and a higher pressure on our side. Things will simply flow into their dimension. I hope.

"The cosmic pressures will be so huge on our side it will literally blow through and into their dimension and with that all the bugs we have loaded into Tammy's body, along with the pressure wave that will pass from this universe into theirs will be of such a magnitude their facility will not be able to withstand it.

"It should cause a blast effect that will fracture the walls or structural integrity of whatever they work in to the point of breeching it and then the bugs are free to do their thing."

I could see the level of concern coming up in Reg's eyes. "What will happen on this side?"

That was the big question. The one that was unknown and could well be the decision maker as to what we eventually do. "Reg, I'm not sure."

He kept pressing the point and

continued. "How do you know that will happen?"

I thought about that and my observations so far tells me that is the best indicator of what will happen and I knew if we could get into their dimension and get a look at it then we should be able to make a better and more accurate prediction.

So, I addressed his concerns, "First of all it's the gargoyles. They are small in size compared to us. Yet, they are fast as lightning. That tells me their environment is under a greater stress than ours. "They are small because of the gravitational forces they must live under. They have powerful bodies in order to function in that gravity.

When we dump that stuff into their portal it will be like a vacuum, pulling everything fed to it into their dimension and spreading it far and wide in just hours. Once started, they cannot stop it until the portal closes or the pressures equalize. We will close the portal before that happens.

"What we need is a means of feeding as much of our chemical weapons through that portal as we can in a short period of time. We cannot leave it open for an extended period of time. We must be careful."

He was nodding his head in agreement in regards to keeping the portal open. "What happens if it's left open too long?"

That was an obvious question and I was sure he would not like the answer. "The vacuum will be so strong it will rip the barrier between the two dimensions wide open and then we will all die. It could almost be like a chain reaction going into the other dimensions that they control. God only knows how many living beings would be killed just for the sake of getting the Cyclers."

He sank back in his chair and looked at me. "Larry, I need a time layout. How long for the portal to be open? How much chemical weapon is to be infused into their dimension? And, when are we going to do this?"

Good, he was still heading in the right direction. "Reg, I would guess, right now, we cannot leave it open more than twenty to twenty-three seconds. I will be able to refine that before we make the move. The amount of chemical is harder to say. I would say not less than five thousand gallons, more if possible.

As far as when, that would depend on how soon we can set the mirrors up and capture us a gargoyle, then set up the video and audio implants and send the first one of them back and get a look at our real adversaries. Once we have that intelligence, then I think we would be ready within days. Remember the planetary alignment happens shortly and we must coincide with that happening.

"We can start the production of the chemicals now and get that all ready. We will need a delivery system as well; some means of injecting that stuff into the other dimension through the portal. Once that is done, we can then send the second one back and in that way block the portal open and start the injection."

He was deep into his thought about this project. "Aren't you worried about more of them coming through while the portal is open?"

Another good question and one I was ready for. "No, because the injection will be under high pressure and they probably could not enter against that level of force. Second, we would still have the blocking mirror in place and holding them out.

"Do you have anything else at this point?"

He sat forward and looked at me. I could see he was ready. I sure as hell was ready myself. "No, Larry I think we are ready to get started."

So now we needed to address the chemical issue and that was going to be a big one. "All right, let's get the manufacturing of the chemicals going, the sooner the better. I don't think we need to address the necessity of tight security in that process."

He nodded and got up and headed for the door while looking back. "It will be tighter than anything we have ever done before."

I knew it would be and now shifted my attention to the major project before me. "All right, I personally want to get going on the capture of a gargoyle and the sooner the better on that as well."

As we walked out of my room, we were still getting things organized and job tasks worked out. Reggie had things going already. "In the situation with the mirrors they have been moved into a secure room and are currently being bolted down to the floor and the rail system is being installed. They advise me they will be ready by morning."

That was great news and I knew we were on our way. "Great, then tomorrow we will go fishing and see what we can catch."

Reggie smiled. "I hope it's a big one.

Well, something we can brag about."

It then came to me. I didn't like it but it had to be tended to. "Now, we have one other worry."

Reggie asked. "What's that?"

I almost didn't want to say it, but it needed to be worked out. "It's Mark Manning and the two young girls that were sitting with Tammy when I came in and sat down with her. We need to make sure of their position on this situation. Are they with us or still under the influence of the Cyclers?"

Reggie seemed to sag at the thought there were others who could be under the control of the Cyclers. "Right, I forgot about that. That will be easy enough to work up. We'll give them polygraph tests that will screen them out quickly and efficiently. As far as Mark is concerned, I have little doubts that he is clearly under the Cyclers control. We will give him a chance, but I'm almost a hundred percent sure he is."

That caught me by surprise. "Polygraph test? Why didn't you use that system on me or Tammy? It could have stopped this entire situation before it even got started."

"Because we don't know if it works or not, but they don't know either. If there is nothing wrong, they will take the test and think nothing of it. If there is something wrong, they will resist the test and then try to fake it." He picked up the phone and called his security captain and advised him what to do and to get it done as soon as possible.

Wow, Reggie could be one heck of a devious guy. He was playing their guilt and insecurities against them and in all probability it will work. "Good move Reg and you call me devious."

That afternoon all three people were offered the test and Mark refused. He was then placed back in a cell. As I watched him, I turned to Reggie, "Kill him."

Reggie wasn't prepared for that. Oh, he knew that if they proved to be under Cyclers control that they would have to be eliminated, but his reaction was that of surprise. "What?" He hadn't expected the bluntness and directness of the comment and the finality that was in it.

I said and knew that I needed to follow up with some reasoning for him. "I said, kill him. Watch him, he's in direct contact with the Cyclers and they know something is up. Kill him and do it now."

I knew I couldn't do it so I had to get

someone else to do it. I had already seen Reggie kill Tammy with one blow and felt he could probably do the same with Mark. All I knew is it had to be done and done now. Reggie entered the cell and as he did Mark sat up on the cot he had been laying on and looked up at Reggie. He started to say something when Reggie walked up to him and hit him with a single blow, putting him down for the count.

The two girls were run through the polygraph and both passed with flying colors. As it turned out both young women were mathematicians and both wanted to get involved in the preparations for the invasion of the Cyclers dimension.

They were eager to get going and we went to work. It only took us about three hours before we had all the figures done and turned them over to Reggie and his people to get the production going.

Next was the preparation for the capture of the gargoyle. We went to the capture room and watched as they tested the track and locking system for the reversal mirror. Even the testing phase was critical in that they could not let the mirrors be uncovered for even a second while doing the test. Still, they had to be done. How much shock could the mirrors take in the opening and closing speeds we wanted them to function at?

By meal time all the preparations for the capture were complete and ready for tomorrow. The reversal mirror was tight in place and the capture room was locked down tight as well. We were ready for one of the most bizarre events in all of mankind's history, the capture of an actual gargoyle. Not only that, but the capture of an alien gargoyle from another dimension.

After our dinner, we again sat down and went over all we had done in preparing the capture room and mirrors for the next day. Every detail was reviewed to ensure no mistakes would happen when we finally got that thing in the room.

It was then I noticed Hanna standing off to one side. I walked over to her and she looked at me and started to tear up. "What's wrong Hanna?"

At first, she said nothing, just looked at me in a way that was hard for me to stand there and see. You know the hurt puppy or sad eyed puppy look. "I heard about Tammy, she was my friend, why did they have to do

241

that to her?"

I put my arms around her and held her as she seemed to just melt. I could see it had been hard on her and she needed to let things go. After a few minutes I looked at her. "Are you going to be all right?" I explained to her what had happened that brought this thing to a head. I held nothing back because I wanted her to fully understand just what was going on and what it meant to everyone in this facility.

She listened intently taking in every word I said. Finally, she appeared to be satisfied with my explanation. It did not change her feelings toward Tammy, which was just the way I felt as well. Finally, she said. "Yes, but I want to help. I want to do something."

That was what I wanted to hear, it told me she still hurt, but she understood. "Good, I could use an assistant." With that we went to work.

We double checked the mirrors and their tracking system and they worked perfectly, they were strong and powerful. The remote monitoring equipment was installed. We had four cameras for complete redundancy. The same was true for the audio systems.

The system for immobilizing the creature once it was captured was working and had been checked and double checked. We had no real idea as to what would put that thing down, so we had set up a system that could introduce six different chemicals into the room.

The recovery team was also armed with every conceivable weapon and we felt sure one of them would do the job. We had determined a live capture was not what we wanted after all. We needed this thing dead and whole. Everything depended on it. Nothing else could progress until we had it down and, in the morgue, so the cameras and sound equipment could be loaded onto or into it.

It was at that time the doctor came into the dining hall. He walked over to Reggie and me and sat down. "Well, I just finished the autopsy on Tammy."

Reggie put his fork down and pushed himself back from the table, "And?"

The doctor looked at the two of us and then turned directly to Reggie. "She is human one hundred percent."

We sat there not really knowing what to say or fully understanding what he had just said. Reggie sat there letting what the doctor had said settle in. "She is not a redesigned gargoyle or something like that?"

The doctor shook his head and continued. "No, she is all human. However, I can tell you she has had surgery on her head, under the hair line. We went into her head and found an implant."

That one got to me and I could see Reggie reacting to what the doctor had said. I felt myself flush, almost getting up and walking out. She was not a gargoyle or whatever else. She was Tammy and they had loaded her up with a device.

Reggie asked "What kind?"

"Well, we're not sure. It has no radio capabilities we could find. But it did have a power source built into it and it was wired to her brain. If I were to guess I would say it was a control device, but not a transmitting device." The doctor sat there giving us time to digest what he had just related to us.

Not a transmitter, but a control device. I was screaming in my mind, damn them anyway, but that cleared up everything and we knew a lot more about how they work. "Good, that gave us just what we needed. They took her and wired her to control her and sent her to us. They did not have the ability to build in a tracking system and that could be because of our dimensions differences from theirs.

"All right, then we can use her and the gargoyle both. If we hit them with both bodies, they will not discover the video and audio equipment until we've had time to collect some data. We may get as much as fifteen minutes or so."

Reggie raised his hand about shoulder high and waved it back and forth. "Larry, that's not going to work."

"How is that?"

He then continued. "We need her to load the chemicals in for the attack, so we can't send her back if the initial job is to gather intelligence not launch an attack. No, we need to send the gargoyle back with the audio and video feeds and let them do its job."

I knew I was wrong and had not been thinking straight. "You're right. I'm jumping the gun. We need to save her for the primary attack and use the gargoyle for the intelligence attack.

"That's it, we have everything in place and we can commence first thing in the morning. We'll put the base on alert at eight hundred hours and we can start the baiting at ten hundred hours. If we are lucky, we should have something in the trap by noon."

By this time, we were back in the control room and Reggie was leaning on a desk. He looked over at me. "Yes, then what do we do?"

I kind of smiled and sat down on the desk and folded my arms. "That my dear Reggie we will find out tomorrow, we'll either have a tiger by the tail or a fine specimen to work with."

We called it quits for the night and I headed back to my room. As I entered the room and looked at the bed, I felt a sharp pain in my chest. They had destroyed that woman with their technology. I simply enjoyed being with her and then this all happened. She knew she was a problem. I saw that when she told me she was sorry as she died. She had no control over her actions. They took that away from her and for that they will pay.

I couldn't go to bed that night. Not with the memory of her dying in the same bed. I walked over to the lounge chair and sat down and looked at the bed. I was glad it had been Reggie and not me. I knew we were going to have to kill her. They left us no choice. Still, it hurts and probably will for some time.

Well, our time is now coming and we will take great pleasure and go to great pains in dealing everything back on them. I laid my head back and reviewed our preparations. Next thing I know it's seven in the morning and I'm wide awake and ready to go.

I managed to take a shower and put on some clean clothes before going to breakfast. This meal was important. We needed to eat a good full breakfast so we would be fully awake and ready to work. I knew with myself I needed to eat before a major issue day and this was a major issue day for sure.

By the time I got to the control room they had the lights on and all the monitoring equipment warmed up and on line. As I sat there and looked at the monitor, I could see the dual mirror assembly up against the wall on the far side of the room. The stationary mirror was bolted to the wall by means of a frame made of half inch steel angle iron, welded at the corners.

Right then Hanna came into the control room and took the seat behind me. She reached out and touched my shoulder. I turned and seeing her smiled and then handed the schedule tracking papers and we settled into start the run.

It would take a ton of explosives to bring it away from the wall. The moveable mirror was mounted in a similar frame and was also sitting on a double track with full support framework behind the mirror. The frame was on rollers designed with track guides to hold the mirror and frame in place. It was heavy and powerfully strong. Nothing was going to move it unless we wanted it to move.

Everything else in the room was elephant proof. By that I mean an elephant couldn't do any harm to anything in the room no matter what. It was a fine piece of engineering and construction. They did themselves well on that job.

I looked over at the reverse camera so I could see the wall opposite the mirror. We had set it up with a video showing the inside of an office. It was a fake layout, but they had to have something to look at and see before they would commit to sending a gargoyle through. I was pleased, it looked real.

Reggie came through the door and walked over to me and sat down. "Well Larry, how are things looking."

"Just fine Reg, just fine. The engineers

and mechanics in just a few days had achieved everything we had wanted for this facility."

It was about five to ten minutes when I looked around and noted everyone was in their place and ready to go. All we needed to do was give them the go ahead. Reg looked at me. "Shall be get started?"

This was it, the moment we had been working for and we were about to take our first step in hitting back at the Cyclers. I looked over at Reggie and nodded my head. I then looked at Hanna and smiled. "Go for it."

He looked over at the lead engineer and nodded his head and the engineer reached out and pushed the green button on his control panel and sat back.

I looked at the monitor and saw the movable mirror start to move to the right and roll away from the stationary mirror. This was it. No turning back and no second guesses. It either worked or we were dead. I think everyone in the control room stopped breathing at the same time. It was dead silent in there and only the hum of the electronics could be heard.

It had been sometime since the last time I had seen one of these things come into this world. I sat there watching the mirror's surface and waiting for the telltale surface movement that preceded their entry.

Chapter Nine

CAPTURE

The time had come to push the button and move the mirrors apart. Reggie had given the go ahead and the tech had hit the green button. The mirror started moving to my right and slid over against the wall and came to a stop.

Everything came to a stop. We watched the open mirror like it was the coming of the end of the ages. Just then I saw a small flash in the lower right-hand corner of the mirror.

I reached over and touched Reggie. "They're there."

I looked back at Hanna. "You ready?"

She smiled and held up the button and nodded at me.

He looked at me and then back at the mirror and then to me. "How do you know?"

I pointed toward the monitor. "I saw the flash in the lower corner, to the right. I have seen this before and knew it was them. I think it means they are observing the area on the other side of the mirror. Hope the fake office projection works."

We sat there for what seemed like hours when I noted a disturbance on the surface of the mirror.

This was it and my guts were literally flipping end over end. "Reggie, they're coming. See the ripple in the mirror."

By this time, he was almost on top of the monitor looking at the mirror. "Yeah, I did this time. Get ready everyone we think we're going to have company."

The mirror surface rippled again and then it became quiet.

It was something to see. A solid surface if we tried to go through it would simply break, but here, with them coming through from another dimension, the mirror acted differently. It entered my mind. *How could that be? How a material object in this dimension could be changed in that way.* For the time being it would have to remain a mystery. I made a mental note to investigate this process in the future. It was still trying to work its way into my thought pattern when my attention refocused on the mirror.

It wasn't more than thirty seconds later when the surface of the mirror erupted and a body came sliding through and into the capture room. As the creature moved away from the mirror and into the main area of the room, I got ready to have Hanna hit the close button. When I did, all hell was going to break loose and we were going to see a show of a lifetime.

The creature slowed down and stopped and just looked around. Just as it hesitated, I nodded and Hanna hit the button and the movable mirror shot back into place and the locks slammed closed. It was on the back of the mirror almost too fast to see, but it missed. We had our capture. Now all we had to do was kill it.

I sat there watching the creature as it moved down off the back of the movable mirror. It then went to the middle of the room and started looking the place over. I could almost see it thinking. I was convinced this creature was a highly intelligent thing. Its eyes were searching around the room for anything it could use or take advantage of. It made me hold my breath waiting for it to find a solution to its capture.

I looked around the control room and everyone there was in a state of shock. None had seen one of these things before. The truth shot through them like a bullet. This was the real thing and the Cyclers were out there. The reality of the whole situation hit them hard.

Several got up and ran out the door. One young woman couldn't make it to the door as she started to throw up and wet herself at the same time. Hanna reached out and put her hand on my back and put her head against it.

I looked at Reggie. His face was gray with disbelief. I reached over and put my hand on his shoulder. He looked at me, but could say nothing. "I understand Reg. It's something totally unreal when you see it for the first time."

For him it was the second time and it reminded him of the first and the terror that took place then. You could see the hate well up in him.

I cautioned him. "That is not a Cycler. Reg, I think these are the attack forces for the Cyclers. It is my hope when we send that thing back, we will get a good look at the Cyclers and then know the whole truth about them."

An hour had passed and the creature had done nothing but pace back and forth like a caged animal. Finally, one of the medical staff asked. "Are we going to kill that thing soon?"

Reggie looked at me and I nodded my head. "We might as well get it over with."

You could see the glint in Reggie's eyes as we made the final preparations to hit it with enough gas to take it out. He had waited a long time for this moment and no one was going to take it away from him, "All right everyone, time to put this thing away."

The medical staff moved to their desks and the preparations were made to euthanize the creature. We had considered the fact this creature was a biological being. We were sure it was carbon based, that would make a difference in how we euthanized it. It left the process as to what would actually kill it up to guess work, so the medical staff had put together several methods of carrying out the kill process.

They started with the obvious and applied gas. Yes, the same gas I was considering for this base, arsenic. The gas hit the chamber slowly, filling the entirety of the room. The creature knew something was going on, but did not seem to be affected by the gas. We waited several minutes and finally it started to show signs.

The medical examiner then stated our dosage was too low and we needed to increase the amount, so we doubled it. That made a difference, but it was not putting it down. It was not fighting or running around, but it was not going down either. It was showing all the classic signs of arsenic poisoning, but not going down.

Then they doubled the dosage again and this time it started to have a direct impact on the creature. Clearly it was a carbon-based animal and in less than fifteen minutes it was down. We kept pumping gas into the room for the next twenty minutes. At the end of that time, we pumped the room clear and then sent in a robot to check on the creature's vitals.

After about ten minutes the medical examiner advised it was in fact dead. A team then went into the room and made sure it was dead and not just playing games. Once confirmed they then started sterilizing it using steam and anti-bacterial sprays to ensure no unwanted foreign bugs came into the room from the other side. Teams of cleaners entered the room to ensure everything, including the creature was washed down.

They placed the creature on a table and went to work conducting the autopsy and taking samples to be placed in glass jars with formaldehyde, again to ensure there was no contamination.

An implanting of the video and audio bugs in its head followed. That took another hour and a half and finally we had a signal from both bugs and the job was done. It was ready for the return process to send it back to the Cyclers.

As the medical staff examined the creature, they determined it lived in a high gravitational area or dimension. Its physical layout was designed to withstand much more pull on its body than we are. That explained its ability to move and respond so fast in our dimension.

However, its eyes were not like ours. They were designed and made for low light levels. That explained it's moving around in our dimension usually at night. Bright lighting would be a definite disadvantage for it. That would be a defense issue we would need to pay close attention to.

So, the Cyclers dimension was high gravitational with low lighting characteristics, odd to say the least. It was also noted sound would be a problem for them. Under those gravitational conditions sound would not travel that far and it explained the size of its ears. Generally speaking, they were similar to humans with arms, legs, opposing thumbs, and so on. That told us our shape may well be universal.

Its skin was heavy and thick. That told us it needed as much protection from its environment as it could get. The atmosphere in their dimension was probably caustic and could be highly dangerous to us. Protective suits would be required for us if we were to enter their dimension. Right now, no one had a desire to do that.

The question was. Did they all look like this creature? Or was it a soldier or fighter of some kind? They sent the gargoyles to deal with issues here in our dimension, but that did not mean the leaders of the Cyclers look like gargoyles as well. Hopefully by the end of the day that question would be answered.

While the medical team was working on the gargoyle, the mechanical team was setting up the return tube and antenna insertion equipment. Our intent was to place the gargoyle in the tube and when the time came to slide the tube into the mirror, to inject the gargoyle back through the mirror and send a break off hair antenna back with it.

They brought in a third mirror altered so the tube could be run into the incoming mirror while the reversal mirror was still in place. At that, it took the teams four hours, but finally they were done. Everything was set and all we needed to do was double check our work and ensure the re-injection equipment was working.

Everyone cleared out of the room and we were ready to do what needed to be done. The camera and mic were checked one last time and then we were ready. The tube door to the wall mounted mirror was opened and the round mirror in the end of the tube that would push the board and gargoyles body through the mirror was activated. We watched the video monitors and then saw the cross section of the wall mirror appear and then clear it. The hair antenna was working great.

We noted something had taken hold of the board the gargoyle was on and was pulling it through. The round mirror section slid into place in the movable mirror and locked into place. The re-insertion was done and the hair antenna had made it through and then broke off as it was meant to do. We had video and audio and they were clear and clean.

I guess I felt like those guys who worked to get the first astronaut on the moon. When they landed, it was nothing but joy. That's how I felt. We had done it and now we were one step closer to seeing our nemesis.

We knew someone or something had taken control of the body as it came back through the portal into their dimension. The question that hung over us was whether they placed the body in a position where the camera would be able to get the videos we hoped to come up with.

It was all a gamble and one if it paid off, we had them and had them good. We just needed to see the video camera work, even if it was just for a few seconds. Just one simple look at the environment and that would give us more intelligence on them than we had ever had before.

I looked at Reg and he was just sitting there, not moving or making any indication we had succeeded or not. I sat down beside him and looked into his face. At that point he shifted his eyes to mine and I knew he was planning and planning hard. What had started out as data and information collection was now turning to a full-blown assault. He was in a war mode and I knew we would not stop until we had achieved all the goals, we had set.

This was the first time in over seven thousand years mankind had been able to make even the slightest progress in learning something about the Cyclers and we had been the ones to do it. The next few minutes would be the key to our next success or total failure.

Hanna was standing behind me with her hands on my shoulders and massaging me. I looked up at her and she was watching the monitor. There was a look in her eyes that told me she had taken a step forward in her life that would change everything for her.

Chapter Ten

FINAL COUNT DOWN

How do you prepare yourself for something no one had ever seen? We sat there stone cold and frozen in place. What was before us was something so bizarre and unbelievable no one could speak.

It was a room I was sure of. The view from the video camera in the gargoyles eye was looking straight up and that was a ceiling, but something I had not expected. It was more like a rock cave ceiling. It was rough and cracked in all directions. The color was a deep ruddy green. Not anything I was expecting.

Then I saw something in the periphery of the cameras view. It was there just for a second and then moved off. Then I saw a hand reaching across the face of the gargoyle. Yes, it was a hand. There were four fingers and a thumb. The hand was short from wrist to tip of the fingers. Almost like a child's hand. The fingers were short and stubby and I could see no finger nails.

The color was a pale yellow, and I mean yellow. I saw no material such as a shirt sleeve or something like that. Just then the top of a head appeared and it was bald, I mean no hair at all. Then I realized neither did the hand or arm have any hair.

They were moving the gargoyle and board off the platform and onto the floor at which time we saw the tables or what we thought were tables around that location.

Then we saw it. Its legs were short and had no knees. Where the legs met the body, it spread out in the form similar to an egg with the wide part of the egg being where the legs were attached. The legs were short and stocky and well muscled. On top was a head that appeared to just pop out of the small end of the egg and form a dome. There was no neck. They were about three feet tall.

Skin texture was odd. It appeared to be smooth with little or no wrinkles. As I sat there, I noted it had no clothes on at all. There were no nipples on its chest area and no sexual organs were seen. For the most part it was like looking at an egg, a yellow one at that.

Its mouth was in the same location as ours and the eyes again relatively the same layout. They had stereo vision for sure. The arms also popped out of the egg body and they were stocky just like the legs. They had elbows and then hands. That was it. Ugly little things you would just as well like to forget about. Again, they had no clothing? Well forget about it, they had none on and frankly it wouldn't have helped in the slightest.

Reggie reached over and turned the sound up. We could just faintly here a garbled noise come through. After watching them for a few minutes we could tell it was coming from them and it must have been their form of communications. Their mouths were moving and it was in sync with the sound. Gees they don't have teeth either.

As they moved the gargoyles body around, we got more and more looks at their control center. One wall appeared to be covered with equipment, possibly tracking or computer equipment. The floor appeared one time and it was smooth as glass and appeared to be artificial to me.

By this time a number of these creatures were around the gargoyle checking it out. Finally, they picked it up and carried it some distance from where they pulled it into their control center. As they turned, we saw the portal. It was triangular in shape and appeared to be a flat silver membrane. It looked to be around four feet in size.

As the body was swung around, we could see windows. If they were windows then what I saw outside was a sky that appeared pink in color. I think I saw clouds and they were a redder color. They were moving fast across the window view. That told me they had an atmosphere and one that was violent. It made me think of Jupiter.

Several more creatures moved in around the gargoyle and were looking it over carefully. They had light, but it was a subdued light, I guess you would call it dim.

One creature leaned over the face of the gargoyle and I got a good look at its eyes. No eye lids. That must be a fun situation. Then I noticed a clear membrane slide across the eye. That was just like a lizard's eye.

The design of the eye was not unlike ours except they were probably twice our size and had a large iris that was black as the ace of spades. It clearly was an eye for low light levels. It struck me it was void of any emotion as well.

By this time the sound was increasing. Just by the tone you could tell they were angry and getting madder all the time. They seemed to look at one another and wave their arms while saying something.

Finally, every one of them stopped talking or moving. They seemed to step back and stand away from the gargoyles body. They all appeared to be looking in the same direction, as if someone was approaching them.

A faint shadow came across the body and then a leg and foot appeared. This was a bigger being and this was a being who demanded great respect and obedience from the rest of those there. The body of the gargoyle was on its back and the head tilted to one side.

Just then a hand appeared by the face and it passed over the eye. The hand was much larger than those of the egg-shaped being. This hand had huge wrists and the palm was at least twice that of a human. The fingers were not especially long for the hand, but there were four fingers and a thumb.

We all sat there waiting. I leaned over to Reggie. "Reg, this is a real Cycler. This being is the lord over these creatures and it is in full and total control."

Just then its face came into view. The creature leaned in over the gargoyle and looked closely at its face.

There are times in one's life when any attempt to clearly and accurately describe something is clearly beyond one's ability. There are just not enough words to fully and clearly communicate what one was seeing. This was one of those times.

Generally speaking, this creature was probably around five feet tall. It was heavily muscled, so muscled it made it appear to be stocky and heavy set.

Overall, its body's general design was much like ours. Its eyes were hard and lacked any form of compassion. It was a creature accustomed to being in a superior position and totally in control.

I got a short view of the side of its face and noted its ears were probably twice ours in relationship to its head. Its mouth looked like a slit across the face in roughly the same position as ours. I saw no lips. I noted no nose, as we would expect a nose to look like. When it moved its mouth, I saw it did not have teeth, but actually had a solid plate across both the top and bottom of its mouth.

As the being examined the gargoyle it seemed to know just what it was looking for. It brought its finger to the eye and pressed in on it completely covering the lens of the camera. It then pulled its hand back and apparently pulled the gargoyle upright and looked close into the camera eye. It leaned back and appeared to smile, at least I think it's what it did and then it took its finger and punched into the gargoyles eye and the camera went dead.

Reggie reacted as if someone was trying to punch him in the face. He turned to me. "What the hell was that?" Pointing at the monitor at the same time.

I couldn't help myself; I had to laugh at his reaction. "That my dear Reg was an actual Cycler."

He looked at me and then back at the monitor. "I thought the egg like guys were the Cyclers."

I shook my head. "No, they responded to this being like it was superior to them and in charge. I have a firm belief this was a

Cycler and they are formidable. That my dear friend is one hell of a being and it could care less about what it has to do to maintain control over us. The problem is this give us no idea as to how many or what their population is."

Reggie sat back. "OK, now what?"

My mind was charging ahead trying to build a better understanding of what we had just seen. "I would say we need to plan our next move. We still have Tammy's body and it is ready to carry out its mission. We just need to make the biological virus we are going to hit them with and then send it through as well."

Reggie stood up and turned toward the door and then back to me. "Larry, can we still do that? The way the big thing acted; he knew what was going on." The look on his face was one of puzzlement and concern. The sight of that creature had really hit him.

I got up and followed him away from our positions. "Yes, he knew we were trying to find out something about them and that's as far as it goes. When I looked into its eyes, I saw a creature with no feeling at all. If ever there was a psychopath this was the king of them all. It was amusing to him we would

269

attempt to look in on him and it was just what we want it to think.

"We're too stupid to match ourselves against them and their intellect. It makes no difference where in the universe you are, there is always someone or some group of individuals who feel they are above and beyond you in intelligence and abilities.

That thing had nothing but contempt for us and it is the way I am going to treat it. We own that thing and it's going to find out in short order."

I walked on past Reg and out of the control room and over to the biological lab. As I went in the door the head of the lab was just coming out of his office. "Hi Larry, what can I do for you?"

I had so many things going on in my head I had to stop and think for a few before responding. "Teddy, you can give me the meanest biological virus mankind can produce. It's got to be something fast and a hundred percent deadly. Got anything like that."

Teddy stood there looking at me and then an odd smile built itself across his face. "Larry, I think you're mad." He just stood there looking at me like I was some kind of a nut.

I took the bait. "That my friend is exactly what I am and I am now ready to kick some ass. What have you got?"

By this time his smile was so big I thought it may split his face right there in front of me. He continued to look at me, then turned and walked over to the freezer and pulled out a red labeled bottle. "Larry, there is nothing like this anywhere on Earth," as he raised the bottle up toward my face. "The day you asked for us to make it I knew I would be able to give you something that will kill any living organism anywhere. If it is organic, it is dead."

He had not said anything that would clearly give me the confidence I needed to use it. "All right, how many individuals will that bottle kill?"

Teddy got serious and set the bottle down on the table top and leaned over it. "Larry, that is the beauty of this stuff. It is self replicating and once released it will continue to grow and expand until nothing is left. It would devour an entire planet in less time than it takes to build a house. It is non-stoppable and unforgiving. Anything and everything biological will die, period."

I couldn't help myself. I felt the smile run across my face. This was too good to be true. It was more than I could ever ask for. "you're telling me we don't dare drop even a single atom of this stuff. That if we do it will destroy all life on Earth?"

Teddy stood there looking me in the eye. This man was letting me know this was the dooms day weapon and it cared not one iota as to who it killed. "That's right. We have to get this stuff into her body and then get her body into the injector and then inject it into the other dimension without any of it getting out."

I knew we were walking a tight rope and it was our responsibility to handle this stuff carefully and responsibly. "There is no antidote for it?"

Teddy held up his hand to silence me before I went any further. "Well, I didn't say that. I said it is self-replicating and fast, so fast we may not be able to implement the antidote fast enough.

"It is actually a neutralizer that will shift the virus to a neutral state and make it dormant. We can then cancel it with the antidote."

Every time he opened his mouth this

thing got that much more complex. "So, our problem is the speed in which this stuff works?"

Teddy picked up the bottle and returned it to the freezer. "That's right. I would say if you had a syringe of antidote in your hand with the needle against your skin and I then opened this bottle, it would get you and kill you before you could push the needle into your arm.

"At that we were able to develop a neutralizer that drives the virus into a dormant state and then we can handle it at our leisure."

All right, if the virus is so fast and the antidote could not be applied fast enough to stop it, what good was a neutralizer anyway? "You're sure of that?"

He took a deep breath and then walked over to me. "Well fairly sure."

That simply was not good enough. "No, Teddy, I want you to be a hundred percent sure, got me."

He could see my concern, but I had not given him the opportunity to complete his statement. "Larry, if we fill the chamber where the injector is at with neutralizer that will do the trick. If any of the stuff gets free inside the room, it's dead. That my friend I will guarantee.

"Now, once the injection is done, we need to seal those mirrors together and then seal the room off and keep it filled with the neutralizer. Then and only then will I feel we have blocked any of it from getting free. When we are done loading her body with the stuff, it will be the last of it on this Earth."

Finally, I was beginning to understand what these scientists had achieved and it was impressive. "Now that's some good thinking. I would hate to win the battle and lose the war all together.

"All right, prepare it for loading into her body, but keep it here until we are ready."

It was all set and we had the ultimate weapon I had been hoping for. I turned to leave and looked back at him. He was smiling at me and replied. "We will have her ready and done in no time."

With that I walked back to the control room. They were busy in the capture room getting ready for the injection of Tammy's body into the other dimension. Everything was there and ready to go.

I sat down by Reggie and he turned to me. "Ready?"

He was tired and was showing it. "Yes,

we're ready. Larry, what is your complete take on this main creature, the one who killed the camera?"

I thought I had already told him, but went into it again for him. "I've thought about that Reg and I have come up with a few things.

"By the appearance of the feet and legs I would say it was around four and a half to five feet tall. It was bipedal like us, but its legs and arms were short and stocky. Its hands were large, but the fingers were short and stout. Overall, I would say it was a powerful body built for the burden of a strong gravitational field.

It's face? Well, that was just ugly. Yet, its eyes were cold and calculating. There was no feeling in those eyes. It was the perfect psychopath, absolutely no emotions what-so-ever. It was intelligent though. I would say it was extremely intelligent and it knew how to use it and gain an advantage with it."

"Larry, do you think it knows what we're about to do?"

I placed both hands on the desk top. That was a good question. "I would say it knows we are up to something and its guard will be at full preparedness for anything from us. I don't know if it figures we will try what we are getting ready to do. I hope not, because if it does, we'll see the world destroyed this day.

"I think we need to give them a little time. I don't know if their time table is the same as ours or not. Do they function on a minute and an hour concept and if they do how long is their day, twenty hours or thirty hours? So, I propose we wait six hours and then make the insertion.

"Next, I want the capture room blacked out. Paint every wall black and leave nothing that can reflect or generate light in the room. We then place Tammy's body in the injector and seal it in and then leave the room and let it rest until the six hours are over."

He was already moving as I finished. "All right, I'll get them to painting the room now."

He picked up the phone and called the head of the maintenance crew and told him to get it painted in the next hour. They set to it and completed the task within the hour leaving just one video camera on and focused on the injector door.

I called the biological lab and told them to load Tammy up and move her body into the capture room and place her in the injector. That task was completed in about sixteen minutes.

We still had no idea what the change in the environment would do to her body. It could be so abrupt it could cause the virus vial to break prematurely and not have the ability to fully enter their dimension. Yet, if we just got a drop in there, it should work. All was now ready for the final move.

The table she was on was set up with a camera mounted on a solid stand. The camera had a wide-angle lens and it was self cleaning. Once she was injected the virus container would rupture and the chemical would escape into their atmosphere and then do its thing.

We would be able to see the response of the creatures on that side and hopefully monitor its spreading out for a period of time. At that point I had no idea as to what was going to happen. It crossed my mind they may have a dooms day machine hooked up to our dimension that will activate and wipe us out as well. Whatever the case, we would be free of them.

I turned to Reggie. "If this thing works and it does knock them out, what do you think will happen here on Earth?"

He sat there a minute. "I don't know Larry. It could be that nothing happens. Their machines could just keep on running us and we see no difference.

"Or, the immediate release of all six billion of us could result in any number of things. Everyone could go crazy and start tearing ourselves apart. Or, all the real nuts in the world would build their power bases and start any number of wars vying for world domination. Or, our whole economy would collapse and push the whole of the world back to the 20th century.

"It's hard to say, but I'm sure there will be a repercussion. I don't think the sudden change will impact us nearly as much as it does the rest of the world. Those of us from across the world have looked at this issue a number of times and agree it will probably be up to us to give the leadership the rest of the world will need until such time the world has regained it initiative."

We noted all the preparations had been done and the capture room was now sealed and the injection was ready to go. We had twenty-five minutes to the injection point. People were gathering around monitors all over the base and the people in the control room were doing their final prep for the injection.

The last action taken was to fill the capture room with neutralizer to ensure the virus did not get free in the room and ultimately our dimension.

Everything had come down to this point in time, this moment when the human race took its revenge or came to an end. Surely if they survived this attack, their retribution on this world would be swift and final. That was one thing I didn't even want to think about.

I could just visualize every mirror in the world suddenly erupting with gargoyles and lordships coming through. It, would-be all-out war and I was fairly sure they had the advantage.

Finally, Reggie gave the project director the go ahead and he started the final countdown at five minutes. As I sat there, I thought about Tammy and me spending time together. It was special, until I found out she was one of them, I was so happy.

Now we were sending her to do a job I thought she was going to be helping me do. Over the years how much terror and hurt have these beings generated here in our dimension? The loss of life and numbers of injured go into the many, many millions across the world, just for the sake of their being able to control our world.

What was their reason for this attitude, this drive to control? Were we over reacting? Is this the right thing to do? Everything seemed to fall in on me at that moment. I was worn out and my mind was in a state of near collapse.

I knew we could not continue to live this way. Any world should have the right to direct and run itself without the interference from outside. If we fail and die off, that is our problem, our doing. We all have an equal risk in this universe and it's up to each social structure to succeed or fail. We don't need their help.

I looked at the clock and it was at thirty seconds and then it hit me. I reached over and hit the red button and the alarm went off. Immediately the countdown stopped at twenty-three seconds.

Reggie looked at me, "Larry, what the hell are you doing?"

"Reg, it just came to me out of the clear and we had almost fallen for it. This thing is a trap and we almost fell into it."

Reggie was shaking his head and

starting to stand up. "No wait, why are you stopping it?

"Reg, it's a set up."

I was sure I had this one nailed down. If we pushed her through the portal all hell was going to bust loose.

He literally froze where he was at. "What do you mean set up?"

I reached out and placed my hand on his shoulder. "Reg, the window behind the mirror is no longer there."

Everyone in the room reacted and Reggie was starting to shake, not from fear, but from anger. "What?"

I was shaking, knowing full well we had almost finished ourselves off. "They closed it as soon as they discovered the video and audio equipment in the gargoyle. That is what that thing was smiling about.

"If we slam Tammy's body through the portal it will hit a solid wall and explode and we'll have all that crap in her to contend with."

Reggie sat back down. "Damn, your right. Shut it down people. Do not attempt injection. We have a problem."

I turned to and yelled. "Teddy!"

He came running into the control room.

281

"Yeah Larry, what the hell is going on?"

I knew what I needed to do, but I need to know if everything was ready to go. "Did you set that video probe up?"

"Yes, we did."

Good, we were still in the game. "All right, try to insert it through the portal. Move slowly and see what happens."

The probe entered the mirror and then stopped dead. "It's solid behind the mirror Larry."

I knew it, the creature is not stupid and he took a defensive action that was totally reasonable and right.

By now I was pacing back and forth trying to build a logical picture of the creature on the other side. He damned near got us. "Right, that figures. We almost proved we're too stupid to beat them. Even more important, once they see we caught on then they will take us more seriously."

I could see Reggie was fairly well torqued off. "Well, what are we going to do now?"

I had returned to my seat and was sitting there looking at the monitor. He had us and it meant we needed to make the next move. "Let me think on that for a few. Yes, it had taken the next logical step, a block in the event we would try something like this. It was smart and calculating."

I sat there and it came to me I had to give them something they wanted more than anything else. It had to be so appealing they could not resist complete and total access into this facility. That would be a victory they could not refuse. But, how would that help us get Tammy back into their dimension. The odds are heavy we would not be able to do that. It would be the end. I sat there for a long time.

Reggie was completely depressed. "Larry, we're getting reports of military movements not far from the base, they're going to take us out."

They knew now we were a real threat and this was the Checkmate move they were trying to take. "No, that is not going to happen. There is a way, I don't like it but I think it will work."

He could sense the magnitude of what I was talking about and I could see already he didn't like it. "What's that, Larry?"

I didn't like what I was thinking, but we were at a point where each move had to be a massive and calculated move. We had to give them something they could never refuse or resist, "Me, Reg. Me."

He snapped his head around looking right at me, "You! What do you mean?"

I heard Hanna gasp behind me.

There was a moment there when I was ready to say no that's not what I mean, but I knew it was. It had to be, there was nothing else possible. "Reg, if they had a shot at me, they would take it. The mistake we made was doing our planning with Tammy present. Everything we did was sent to them immediately. She was not just a loved one, she was a direct link to them and they knew who the driving force in this place had become. I was that force.

"They need a certain or special bait that is irresistible, that will fulfill a frustration that has been created. I think I am that bait."

Reggie started shaking his head and slapped his hand down on the desk top. "Larry, you're talking dead here."

I reached out and grabbed Reggie's arm and pulled him close to me. "Hold it and listen, this has got to be worked out and we have to push it. There is nothing else. Reggie, I know what the risk is, but if we don't do something, this place is gone and the world is going to be helplessly under their control forever. I don't like it, but it's something that has to be done."

He was starting to get madder than I had ever seen him. This is the man of total control, the man of deliberateness, planning, cool. "No, there has to be another answer somewhere. I am not going to approve your suicide. That is out of the question. No! If you think you're going to hang that act on my shoulders you've got another thing coming. Damn you Larry, I will not approve, nor will I help."

Crap, he was going overboard on me and I needed to get him under control. "Reg, please, listen to me. I have thought this out and I do not want to die. But I am willing to risk it all to get those things. If I die in the process, to me, it's worth it. Look, I'm no hero. I hate what I am thinking, but I know it will work. So, there is no alternative, we have to risk it."

He sat there and looked at me then seemed to perk up. "Are you saying you do not want to die?"

I smiled at him. "Yes, Reg that is what I am saying."

His demeanor changed again just as fast

as before. "Then you are planning on being bait in the trap and running the risk?"

Now he had it, and we were back on track. "That's right, but I just want to risk it, not actually die."

You could see the questions forming on his face. "How, I mean just what do we do to make this happen?"

Hell, I didn't know, so it was time to play it by ear. "We make it look like we have given up and are now fighting for our lives against the forces outside the base preparing to attack us. In other words, we forget about them and lay ourselves wide open."

If he had hit the brakes any harder, we all would have ended up with whip lash. "Precautions, come on Larry we have to have precautions built into this thing?"

He was right. It would not be smart to just throw myself under the wheels, we needed some planning. "Well, we try and maintain an escape route all the time, for both of us."

Up went his eye brows again, "Both of us?"

I thought to myself. *Come on Reg, I'm not the only one here with any level of drive and authority.*

"Reg, you're just as much a target for them as I am."

He thought for a moment and then nodded. "Right, I didn't think about that."

I now had his undivided attention and set to work. "All right, let's get everyone together in the meeting room. Leave Tammy where she's at for the time being. The countdown is not over, it's just extended."

About six o'clock the following morning the first military contingency appeared outside the facility. It was not an attack force, but more of a blocking force. One designed to keep us in the base and not permit anyone to leave.

We were at a complete lock down and knew it would take much more than what was there to do anything against us. We knew we could withstand a direct nuclear hit, but we probably could not hold out against several hits.

People were fairly nervous over the arrival of the military, but we knew we had time and we needed to continue with our planning. We decided to use Tammy's body as the focal point of our activity and it would take place in the capture room.

We asked for volunteers and then

prepared for our entry into the room. I had Teddy put together a vial of the virus which would then be placed in my pocket when we implemented the plan.

All I would have to do was break it with a blow to the end of the vial. I was then ready to enter the room. My hope was they would come for me and take both Tammy and me. If that happened, we had them.

The plan was to have a unit enter and then take Tammy's body out of the injector tube and move it over against the wall on the opposite side of the room. I then planned on standing by the body with my back to the mirror. They were going to move the reversal mirror off the portal mirror about two thirds of the way and then leave the room.

I was positive they were still watching through the portal, only they were using a small scope and not the whole portal. Everything was set up by eight hundred hours.

They had outfitted me with a set of goggles that had a video camera and audio mic built into it. They also gave me a gas mask that would give me some protection from the effects of the virus. Under my clothes I had a harness hooked to a high strength small diameter cable.

The plan was to try and be captured by the Cyclers and taken through the portal. The mask and goggles were to give me a fighting chance of living in their environment. Once there it was my discretion as to when I broke the vial. I planned on making sure our friend the lordship would be there and when I saw him, I would then break the vial. If they did take Tammy, then I would only have to worry about being retrieved back through the portal. Tammy would take care of the rest of it.

The plan was set and we got ready. In order to make this thing work I needed to be careful to see the equipment was not noticeable at the time they took me. I knew they would send in one or two gargoyles and I had to be prepared for that.

My mind was racing along trying to check on all the basics and ensure we had everything covered. It was all there. Every aspect of the plan had been checked and implemented. All that was left was the final opening of the portal and their coming through to take me.

As I approached the door to the chamber, I felt a hand pull on my arm. I turned and Hanna was standing there, tears running down her face. She moved up against me and wrapped her arms around my body. I wrapped mine around her and held her tight. She looked at me. "You listen to me. I want you to come back to me. Do you understand? Larry, I need you to come back to me."

It was then I felt the surge hit me. She was more than just a helper; she was everything I was fighting for. I held her tighter. "Hanna, thank you for that. Now I know I have something to fight to come back to, I will be back."

Finally, we opened the access door to the room and entered it. The barrier door was closed tight behind us and the crew then went to the mirror assembly and opened the injector and pulled Tammy out. She was placed on the stretcher and rolled across the room and against the wall. I then moved in and positioned myself with the cable attached to the harness under my shirt. The cable in turn was attached to a drum and wench assembly, which was mounted on the floor under the stretcher, for pulling me back through the portal.

The crew then attached two blocks to the mirror rail so the mirror could only be opened to about two thirds of the way and then be held there. It was going to remain in position until I was reeled back through the portal and then it would be slammed shut. That was it, all or nothing. No matter what happened I was going to set a vial off and they were going to be too busy dealing with the virus.

Everyone finally exited the room and the technicians then started pumping the neutralizer into the room. I was by myself standing there beside Tammy. I heard the door close and the bolt slide into place. Then Reggie came on. "You ready Larry?"

The thought passed through my mind, no, how the hell could someone be ready for something like this. "Yes, guess this is it. Did we forget anything Reg.?"

There was a long pause. I mean, we could have carried out the assault and all gone to lunch before he came back. "No, I think it's all covered."

I was running over everything and trying not to talk myself out of this. "How about the military, where are they at right now?"

Again, there was the long-drawn-out pause. "They're still arriving. I think we have maybe two hours before they start their assault on the base."

You ever stood beside a swimming hole knowing full well when you jump there was no going back and cold water was just waiting there to hit you when you landed in it. Well, that was me at this point, I was delaying. "Is everyone ready?"

Reggie remained patient and calm as I built up my courage. "Yeah, they're going to pay dearly to get in here. All right we're going to start the countdown at one minute. You ready for this?"

Finally, there was nothing else I could think of, so it was time. "Go for it."

The countdown started and I was sure this was going to be the longest sixty seconds I had ever experienced. "All right, here we go, sixty seconds and counting."

I felt myself tighten up and knew I had to stay loose and relax. When they hit me, it would be hard and direct. I needed to be prepared for that action.

"Fifty seconds and counting."

I went over my planned moves once inside the portal and in their dimension. I had to concentrate on doing my job. Trying not to let the violence of the moment impact me. If they killed me right off the bat. The vial was set to break on its own five minutes after I entered the portal. If they managed to take Tammy as well, then it's a closed deal. They're dead.

"Forty seconds and counting."

I started deep breathing so I could get all the oxygen into my system I possibly could. I needed to hold out for at least a minute. I had to control myself and be ready for anything.

"Thirty seconds and counting."

Hell, they may not even take the bait. This could be totally for nothing. They may be opting for the military to storm this base and kill us all and thereby eliminating the problem that way.

"Twenty seconds and counting."

All right now start getting yourself ready. I had no idea how long it would take them to determine I was there and alone. I was depending on them keeping a watch through the portal. I was depending on their arrogance to work for me. When looking into the lordships eyes I could see the total contempt and total arrogance he had toward us.

"Ten seconds and counting."

Here it comes. Get ready. I sure as hell hope this works out.

"Five, four, three, two, one."

I heard the mirror slide back and prepared myself for whatever was to come.

If they carried out the assault as they usually did then there would be a period of time between the opening of the portal and the gargoyles coming through the portal as they looked the area over and then prepared the assault. If they were as militarily based as I thought they, where they would take precautions when they came. I had to stay loose and calm. It had to appear I knew nothing was going on and I was deep into my mourning of Tammy.

I was depending on Reggie to keep me informed when and if they took the bait. It felt like hours when Reggie finally said the words that would set everything in motion. "Larry, it's coming through. Get ready. There are two of them and they are about ten feet from you. They are holding off and checking the area out. One is pointing at you and then at Tammy. Larry, they're going to take both of you. Here they come."

I felt the air around me move before it grabbed me. It wrapped its arms around me like a vice. I had to struggle in order the make it think I was surprised. The fact was I was surprised. I did not expect the power of it grabbing me. This thing was stronger than I had anticipated and it made me flash back to my apartment and the near miss I had with one then. I knew as soon as it grabbed me, I would never have been able to fight it.

I saw the other one grab Tammy and we then backed toward the portal. I let the cable drop to the floor and watched it string out. At the portal it would start to come off the reel and I would be in recovery mode.

The gargoyle that took Tammy went through the portal first. Then it was my turn. I remembered when our first attempt passed through and watched for the cross section of the mirror and there it was. I was waiting for the blast to hit me. I had no idea what the change between their environment and ours would it be like.

The environment of the other dimension literally slammed into me. It was hot and humid and the gravitational pull was unbelievable. My whole system sagged at its effects on my body. It took everything I had to remain conscious. It was only ten or fifteen seconds and we were there and the gargoyle dropped me to the floor.

I landed on my side almost in a sitting

position. It dawned on me I was the first person to enter another dimension. Then I thought, no there were others, I was the first here by plan.

I needed to keep my communications with Reggie up and going. They needed to know what was going on. "Reg, you see this?"

No more hesitation, he responded. "Yes, Larry we do. You're not coming through too well, but we got you."

I was concentrating on everything all at once, my breathing, the weight differential, and the communications. I responded, "Same for you Reg, it's hard to hear you. Jack up your volume."

Finally, my eyes focused and I watched the gargoyles move back and away from me, dragging Tammy's body with them. I looked around and recognized the egg-shaped creature. There must have been a dozen of them and they were all standing there looking at me.

The room I was in did appear like a cave except it was not. That must have been their architectural concept. It looked like a cave, but the walls were square and the whole of the room was around fifty by maybe a hundred feet and it was full of electronics. They had monitors along all the walls I could see. The place was a treasure chest of technology.

They had made one huge error when they came for me. They took Tammy with us. She was still loaded and the vial I had in my pocket was nothing compared to what she had inside her. I was able to turn my head and saw the lordship walking toward me.

I was right about its build and size. One thing I did not expect was the impact of its cruelty and appearance. This thing was not in the mood to bargain and was probably going to settle a personal debt with me.

I reached into my pocket and grabbed the vial and pulled it out. It was almost on top of me when I slammed the vial on to the floor and heard it break. That stopped it dead in its tracks. It stood there and looked at me and then at the stain on the floor.

At first, I looked and all I saw was a stain on the floor. "Oh crap, Reg the virus, it's not working. I think maybe you had better retrieve me."

Just then the stain started to change color and spread. I felt the cable go taught on my harness and then I started to move back and away from the lordship and the stain.

The lordship looked at me and screamed in anger charging at me in an attempt to stop me. In his charge he stepped in the stain that by now had turned into ooze that clung on his leg. The virus hit hard and fast. It tore into him and drove itself through his skin and charged into his body. You could see the effect as it devastated him in seconds.

It was slapping at its body and face and the more it slapped the more the virus spread. He threw globs of virus all over the room and some of it hit some of the egg people and they immediately went into convulsions. Withering and trying to wipe the goo off of them. Their cries would haunt me for years, but it's just what they had coming to them.

The room was exploding with goo and parts of egg people all over the place. Tammy's body was coming apart in just seconds, but she had done what she was meant to do. I was transfixed watching everything that was going on.

I remember yelling. "Reggie."

He was right there with me. "Yeah Larry, I'm here and I see what's going on."

I was trying to get back from the explosive expansion of the virus. "The virus, it's faster than I anticipated. Get me out of here now full retrieval speed."

Reggie was trying to be rational. "But that could kill you."

Hell, I was in a situation where I was damned if I did and damned if I didn't. "Reg, if you don't move me now, I'm dead for sure. God, it's already hitting the egg people here and the gargoyles as well."

I felt the cable jerk me and I went flying toward the portal. Just before I got to the portal, I looked at Tammy and she had split wide open and the virus came charging out of her. It was all over everyone in the control center so fast. Just then I passed through the portal and the mirror slammed shut and sealed. At the same time, they were loading the room with neutralizer to ensure the virus had not come into this dimension.

My head was reeling. Had I gotten any of the viruses on me, I didn't know, "Reg, Reggie."

I could hear the excitement in his voice. "Yeah, Larry, I'm still here, you've got to see this."

All I could think of was confirmation. "Is the camera working?"

He was no longer talking, but was

yelling like he was watching a great ball game. "Yeah, it is and you have got to see what is happening. It's a total wipe out. They're trying to get out of the center and when they opened the door the virus shot through it like lightning. We, did it, Larry. It's the end for them."

I was still laying there trying to determine if any of the viruses had gotten on me and in the containment room. "Reg, switch your observation to the military outside and the rest of the world."

I was relieved he heard me with all the yelling and cheering going on in the control room, "Will do Larry. He was still yelling."

As he was doing that I called back. "Reg, is the containment room filled with dormancy solution?"

Almost like it was an afterthought he came back. "Oh, yeah, we did that as you went through the portal.

I felt myself go limp and settled back on the floor and let the stress and chill of the past few minutes slip off of me. We had done it. We had taken the fight to them and they were now paying for seven thousand years of domination over the people of Earth.

I think I may have passed out at that

time and really don't know how long I was out; it could have been seconds or several minutes. I remember coming around as I heard Reggie yelling in my headset. "Larry, wake up. Larry, you need to wake up and listen to me. Are you all, right?

I felt myself crawling up out of the black zone and trying to get my bearing. When he asked me a second time, I was able to respond. "I'm fine Reggie. I think I passed out for a few minutes there, but I'm fine now. What's going on?"

"Larry, by everything we can monitor and learn the other side is a complete wipeout. The military outside the base has come to a complete stand still and I believe they will no longer be a problem.

"We'll be in to get you in about half an hour and then you'll be able to review the tapes and see what has happened."

"Thanks Reggie, I'm ready at any time. Damn I'm tired."

Chapter Eleven

REBIRTH OF MANKIND

By the time I got to the control room they had the monitors filled with scenes from across the world and outside the base. The camera in the Cyclers base was still recording the activity there. It was total chaos. Creatures kept trying to enter their control center and were being knocked down by the virus as fast as they entered. It dawned on me they had no idea what they were dealing with. They had no understanding of germ warfare and it was wiping them out.

Outside the base the military personnel were standing around. Most had dropped their weapons and just stood there. They looked like a bunch of zombies, walking around with no leadership and no idea as to what they should be doing.

We sent a unit out to contact them and they reported back they were acting just like babies. They could not talk and were totally dependent on us trying to care for them.

The look on Reggie's face told the whole story. "Man, this is going to make for some rough times here on Earth."

That I could see without any difficulty. "You better believe it."

By this time everyone was watching the people outside the base. Reggie was saying. "It's almost like, a recording has been wiped clean. Their brains have been cleared of everything, including their personalities. It's a complete wipeout. We are getting reports from the other bases and they are saying the same thing. It was the loss of an entire social structure across the whole world."

I had this strange feeling we may have lost more than we could ever recover from. "Have you any videos of the other bases yet?"

Reggie was busy running through all the other bases data telemetry. "Yes, we have and it's the same with them. The human race is going to be decimated. They report planes have been falling out of the sky. Those on board no longer know how to fly them or anything that has to do with technology. We are estimating in the first week close to sixty percent of the world's population will die, mostly in the third world countries."

I had not expected that. The loss to the Cyclers may have been total, but the loss to us was devastating. "There has got to be some who were living within the system, but were not controlled by the Cyclers. Have we found any?"

After making a number of contacts Reggie started nodding. "Yes, they're reporting there are a lot of them and they are taking over all over the world. We feel within a month we will be back to a semblance of control and life as usual."

"Other reports confirmed all the worlds' governments have collapsed. There are no functioning governments anywhere on the Earth. Everything will have to start new and rebuild our governing systems."

I felt a total collapse coming over me. I was wiped out and all the activity over the past hour nailed me. I then asked. "Do you think there is any danger of the virus getting through any of the mirrors across the world?"

To my relief they had already started checking on that and Reggie reported. "No, those are not accessible. Once the control system is down, the portals are down. They probably shut everything down as soon as the alarm went out of the invasion and the disaster they were facing."

"Reg, were there any of the people in this facility who were under the control of the Cyclers, were there any?" I asked.

"Yeah, we had three. They were in non-critical positions and so were of little concern. When the virus hit and shut the Cyclers down those three just sat down where they were and have been there ever since."

That was another relief point and I sat back in my chair and nodded. "Great, after talking to Tammy I thought there would be many more than just three. That's great news."

I was finally starting to relax and get my head back together. "All right, it's going to be a while before we hear everything that is going on across the world, but that will give us time to plan our next move and work out an implementation process for it. We have our free world, but we made ourselves more work than we would ever really want."

It was then when several of the people in the control center moved and there stood Hanna looking over at me. She didn't look like she was holding up to well. I held my arms at toward her and she slowly walked over to me and sat down in my lap and put her head against my shoulder and wrapped her arms around my body. She stayed there not saying a single word, just holding on.

Reggie was still grinning from ear to ear. "Larry, I never thought we would see the day when I could leave the base front entrance open and feel safe that way, feels good."

I agreed. "Reg, for you I'm sure it's been a long road. I don't think I could have done it myself. You can feel good about the fact you rode it out and you're here today to see the results."

Reggie finally pushed himself back from the desk and turned to me. "What are you going to do Larry?"

Know what, I hadn't even thought about it. "First of all, I am going to sit back and relax for a few days. This thing is just starting and I think it's best for us to sit tight until it's all over."

Then it came to me and I turned to Reggie. "Reg, I would like to have a car so I could go back to Mid Atlantic Group and find out how it came through this situation. If it is void of any leadership, then I think I want to take it over and start rebuilding."

He sat there nodding his head. "That my dear Larry sounds like the right thing for you. Here, take one of our cars and let me know how things work out."

For once in all these weeks I knew exactly what I was going to do. I was single and had no ties so I was free to set out and start building a new and better world. "Great. I'll do that."

I turned and saw Hanna standing there, she had this lost look on her face and I knew, at the least, I needed to address her needs. She walked up to me. "Would you be willing to take an assistant along with you?"

I looked at Reg and he nodded his head. "Sure Hanna, come along. I could use the company and I need a good second hand."

As she stood there in front of me, I got a good look at her eyes and they were not the eyes of an assistant. That was comforting for me and I felt there was definitely something good coming out of this after all.

She stood there watching me and then I told her, "Hanna I think I need you more than I have ever needed someone before."

Three days later we walked out to the car and loaded it up and got in. Reg was standing there and called out. "You two don't be strangers now. Stop by once in a while and see how we're doing."

I looked around the dome remembering my first view of this place. "Will do Reg, will do."

With that we headed off to the Group facilities. I had forgotten what the world looked like in the spring time. It was a beautiful day and everything was bright and wondrous. We sat back and drove the hundred miles home and a new life.

Off in the distance I could see there were a number of fires. Homes and towns were on fire and being returned to the earth they came from. No, mankind would not fare well from this liberation. Too much had been damaged for too long for it to come out a happy story.

Maybe in a few decades' things would start to look more normal, but until then we had a lot of work and a lot of planning to do. I felt I could give much more through the Group facilities than from the base or my own apartment for that matter. To start with I plan on changing the name to something more descriptive of this day and age.

Hanna sat there looking out across the

landscape. She reached over and placed her hand on my knee and left it there. "Do you think we'll ever get it back to the way it was before?"

I looked around at the landscape and the empty cars sitting along the road and nodded my head. "Yes Hanna, we will get it back to what we had before, only it will be much better than it has been. It's going to involve a lot of hard work and some difficult times, but we'll do it I'm sure of that."

As we passed through town, I looked over at my apartment building and noted it was on fire. No reason to go by there and it only brought sad memories anyway so we headed on out of town toward the facility.

I was a little surprised at the condition of everything as we left the city and headed out toward the Group main office facility. As the property came into view it was well groomed and appeared to have been recently mowed. If so then there was someone who had been living and working here while the Cyclers were in control. I made a note to find that person or persons, we would need them.

When we arrived at the Group facilities, there was little left. The campus looked in good shape, but the interior was all torn up.

Papers scattered everywhere and stuff dumped around and left lying.

As we walked the halls toward the executive offices, I thought I heard something. We turned the corner by the cafeteria and saw several grown men and women sitting around on the floor eating cookies and peanut butter out of the jars with their hands. As I walked into the room one looked up and waved at us. It was Stanley Lattamere III and he was completely out of it.

We were now entering a new cycle, the rebirth of mankind and a new future. Those of us who were not controlled by the Cyclers will have to pick up the broken and beaten and help them adjust and hopefully come back to the level they were at when the break came.

After seven thousand years of domination, it won't be easy to bring us back and create a new and more advanced human race. As a being we will have to make our own decisions and pick our own directions and not depend on some unseen being to make them for us.

They were not gods. If anything, they were the epitome of Satan, the dark unseen force who founded its existence in the domination and heartless game playing of the worst kind. If the virus was totally successful, the Cyclers were gone forever and all those other dimensions they controlled will be free and in the same situation we're in.

If the virus was stopped then sometime in the future we will probably be faced with a resurgence of the Cyclers. As a race, we can prepare for that possibility. As individuals we tend to not worry about those things that do not directly impact us. That is for someone else to be concerned about.

So, there you have it. Cyclers turned out to be the real thing and much more of a problem and hazard than even I had thought. I know now it was by chance I was placed in the position I was in.

That happens so often in this life, a person going along minding their own business when out of nowhere something happens and draws them into a situation, they wanted nothing to do with. Then it becomes a life and death issue and you're trapped. You have no way out. I guess that's life.

The only thing I can tell you is, if we become docile and fail to keep a strong vigil, we will become dominated over again, if not by the Cyclers, then by some other aggressive being who cares little about our welfare and everything about their attainment of power and control.

Every time you look into a mirror over your sink understand there may be a being on the other side watching your every move and calculating as to how and when they can again gain control over you and your life. A quarter of an inch of glass and the portal can be opened and you can become the puppet they want you to be.

Hanna and I stayed together from then on. She became my wife and we had a family of four children. The Group Facility became our career and our home. There were lean years and then things started to turn around. We became a recovery school for the re-education of those that were left behind when the Cyclers fell.

Keep a watch. Look to the lower right-hand corner of that mirror. Do you see a small bright flash? They're there, watching and waiting and only time can tell if we're smart enough to recognize the danger when it is staring us straight in the face.

www.ingramcontent.com/pod-product-compliance
Lightning Source LLC
Chambersburg PA
CBHW071107250626
47159CB00002B/634